# How Do You Talk to a Dolphin?

"Jordan?" Mary Beth said. "I need to ask you something. See, I'm a marine biologist, and I'd like your permission to take Zeus out on my boat a few times to participate in an important research project."

"Zeus?" Jordan said. "How come Zeus?"

"Well," Mary Beth said, "I don't know how to say this, but I think he may be capable of . . . well, maybe he's talking. Interspecies communication, actually."

Jordan shrugged. "What's the big deal? I talk to Zeus all the time."

"It *is* a big deal," Mary Beth said. "Because I think Zeus was talking to my dolphin."

**Books by Patricia Hermes**

Be Still My Heart
My Girl
My Girl 2

Available from ARCHWAY Paperbacks

The Cousins' Club: Everything Stinks
The Cousins' Club: I'll Pulverize You, William
The Cousins' Club: Thirteen Things Not to Tell a Parent
The Cousins' Club: Boys Are Even Worse Than I Thought
Heads, I Win
I Hate Being Gifted
Kevin Corbett Eats Flies
Zeus and Roxanne

Available from MINSTREL Books

# Zeus
## and
# Roxanne

A novel by PATRICIA HERMES
Based on the motion picture written by TOM BENEDEK

A
MINSTREL®
BOOK

Published by POCKET BOOKS
New York   London   Toronto   Sydney   Tokyo   Singapore

A MINSTREL PAPERBACK *Original*

A Minstrel Book published by
POCKET BOOKS, a division of Simon & Schuster Inc.
1230 Avenue of the Americas, New York, NY 10020

ISBN: 0-671-00370-4

First Minstrel Books printing January 1997

10  9  8  7  6  5  4  3  2  1

A MINSTREL BOOK and colophon are registered trademarks of
Simon & Schuster Inc.

Printed in the U.S.A.

For Paul, Mark, Tim, Matthew, and Jennifer
and all the special people they have brought into our lives

# Zeus
## and
# Roxanne

# Chapter
# 1

It looked as if Zeus was going to do it. He was surely trying hard enough. He would get that string of kelp. He would.

He raced along the edge of the brilliant blue water of the bay in the Florida Keys, his paws digging into the sandy turf, his tail wagging, his tough little face screwed up with the effort. He pounced and caught the stringy kelp, tossing it in his mouth, shaking it with all his might.

He pretended to be fierce, tossing and leaping, the kelp hanging out of his mouth, while he growled low and deep.

*Click!*

There was a sudden sound from far out in the water.

He stopped.

*Click!*

It came again.

*Click.*

*Blat.*

*Squawk!*

Zeus looked out toward the water of the bay, sparkling in the early morning sunshine.

What made that sound? He listened, very still, the kelp hanging limp now in his mouth.

*Blat! Squawk.*

A creature! It had to be a creature, something live out there, something calling.

For a long moment, Zeus stayed perfectly still, watching. Listening.

The sound came again, louder this time.

*Squawk! Blat!*

And then it appeared, the creature who was making the sounds. It was huge, powerful. Beautiful.

A great, majestic dolphin rose from the bay, throwing sparkling drops of water from its glistening back. *Click! Click!* It threw back its head. *Click. Blat. Squawk.*

Its mouth was open. It was calling to Zeus, and it seemed to smile.

Yes, it was smiling right at Zeus!

Zeus dropped the kelp. He answered it, barking joyfully. Hello, he barked. Hello! Hello!

He leaped up and down at the edge of the waves.

The dolphin stopped calling. It leaped sideways into the air, then dove. Dove and disappeared under the waves.

Gone. The dolphin was gone.

Zeus looked down. The kelp was gone, too.

He stood for a moment, sad. A wave poured in, drenching him.

He shook himself. He looked once more back at the water, but no dolphin, no playmate.

Well, no sense hanging around here. Breakfast time. He had a favorite place to find some special treats in the garbage cans right outside the fenced-in yard in town.

He looked once more at the water, then happily trotted back to town, down the main street, past the fish stores, past the boat yard, right up to the breakfast place.

There were dogs to deal with there, mean guard dogs. Zeus wagged his tail, confidently. No problem. They were back behind the fence. He headed for the metal garbage cans outside the fence. Great treats in there.

The guard dogs saw him and rushed at the fence, barking fiercely.

Zeus looked up. Hey! He hadn't even started on the cans yet. He backed up, took a flying leap, and hit the nearest can.

Nothing. It didn't even budge.

The dogs growled and lunged, beating themselves against the fence. They sounded mean and fierce, not playful like Zeus growling at the kelp. These guys were mean. Zeus didn't care. They were behind the fence, and he was in front of it. And breakfast was waiting.

Once more he leaped at the cans. This time, he landed a well-placed kick. A can toppled over. It hit the next can. That fell over, too. The next one fell, and the next.

Zeus could hardly believe his luck. All the cans! Every one of them, tops off, food spilling out. Fast food. Leftover fast food.

What luck. He raced to the first can, his tongue hanging out, already tasting that food. He stopped.

The dogs. The guard dogs. The big, mean guard dogs. They were *outside* the fence, had dug under, were on his side.

Zeus backed up a bit. Both dogs, huge German

shepherds, stood watching him, snarling, ears back, ready to lunge.

Zeus backed up farther. The dogs moved forward, but they wanted the food, not Zeus. At least, that's what Zeus hoped they wanted.

He backed up yet again. Go ahead, guys, it's all yours.

Then he turned and hightailed it for home as the guard dogs went about their breakfast—a breakfast that Zeus had prepared for them.

Oh well, Jordan would have something for him at home. Jordan was the best. Zeus wagged his tail happily. Or Jordan's father, Terry. Yeah, more likely Terry. Terry always had food to share.

He was almost home. There was Mrs. Rice, toddling down her walk, her fat old tabby cat in her arms, aiming to pick up her morning paper.

Play time!

Zeus tore down the sidewalk, heading for the paper.

Mrs. Rice raced down the sidewalk, heading for the paper.

Zeus bounded at it, but too bad. Mrs. Rice got there first and scooped it up.

Zeus panted up at her.

"Nice try, flea bag!" Mrs. Rice said. "And you think I'm old." She pointed to the house next door. "Go home!" she said.

Zeus went.

He was really hungry now, had worked up a big appetite. But it would be all right. Jordan and Terry, they would take care of him.

4

# Chapter 2

At home, when Zeus plopped down on the porch, Jordan was already at the kitchen stove, a camera slung around his neck, working on his breakfast special. Each time he reached for something, the camera bumped against him or against the stove or the sides of the pan. Once, the camera even got covered with eggs and gook. He had to keep flipping it out of his way, but it was worth the nuisance. He had already gotten some cool pictures of his cooking so far.

He turned, took some burrito-size tortillas, slid them into the microwave, then turned back to the stove.

He leaned over, cracked eggs into a pan that was already smoking—well, maybe burning.

He wrinkled up his nose and tilted the pan away from the heat. Then he swirled the egg mixture around in the pan, stepped back, and quick-snapped a picture.

Perfect. The perfect egg mixture, with the perfect picture of the perfect egg mixture. Jordan loved cooking and picture taking, had been doing both for practically his whole life, his whole ten years.

Jordan leaned around the kitchen door and looked into the living room. Terry, his dad, sat at the keyboard of his digital piano, headphones covering his ears, a frown seeming permanently attached to his forehead. He plinked at a note, stopped to sigh, jotted something down, then plinked some more.

All around him was spread his stuff—stacks of books, CDs, his picture of Mozart, even his fishing stuff. On the wall behind him were pictures that Jordan had taken. And another picture: Jordan's mom.

Jordan sighed. It seemed that ever since his mom died, Terry hadn't been able to get the music to work right. It looked as if Terry had been up all night, working. Again. And he was up against a deadline.

Jordan frowned. Well, food always helped Terry. Especially when he, Jordan, cooked it.

He went back to the microwave, pulled out the tortillas, loaded in the egg mixture from the pan, folded up the tortillas, then carried both plates into the living room.

Terry looked up. "Hey!" he shouted.

Jordan shook his head. Why did Terry always think other people were deaf when he had headphones on?

"Great," Terry shouted again. "Dinner!"

"Breakfast!" Jordan shouted back.

"Oh," Terry said. He took off the headphones and looked out the window. "I knew that," he said, more quietly.

Jordan set the plates down, one in front of him, one by his dad. "You've been up all night again," Jordan said, frowning.

6

"Yeah, I'm sorry," Terry said. He looked at the keyboard. "I know there's a melody in there somewhere. It's just taking me a little time to find it."

Jordan didn't answer. He'd heard that before. It was taking more than just a little time to find it. He nodded to the plate. "Eat," he said.

"Are these burritos?" Terry asked.

Jordan nodded. "Yup. Breakfast burritos."

"Cool. Thanks," Terry said.

Jordan took a big bite of his burrito and waited for his dad to do the same.

Terry took a big, hungry bite. Then a funny look came across his face, and very slowly he began to chew. And chew. And chew.

"Jordan?" he said, a little hesitantly. "What's in this burrito?"

Jordan smiled. His secret formula. "Eggs," he said, and he began ticking things off on his fingers. "Eggs. Refried beans. Onions. Jalapeños. Peanut butter. Pineapple chunks. Mozzarella cheese. Oh, yeah, and"—he smiled at his dad—"lettuce. So it's nutritionally balanced."

Terry nodded solemnly. "Oh," he said.

And then Terry frowned. And sniffed.

Jordan frowned. And sniffed.

Burning. Something was burning.

Jordan jumped up. "I think I forgot to turn off the frying pan!" he shouted, and he headed for the kitchen.

Just as quickly, Terry headed for the porch, breakfast burrito in hand.

Zeus looked up, wagging his tail.

"Good morning, Zeus," Terry said softly. He bent, patted Zeus. "Thank goodness you're here."

He put the burrito down in front of Zeus and patted him again. Then he muttered, "Thank you, thank you."

Quickly then, he went back inside and had just barely slid into his chair when Jordan came back from the kitchen.

"Hey!" he said, looking at his dad's empty plate. "You're finished. I'll get you another one."

But before either of them could move, something else happened, something that made them both stop and frown. It wasn't a smoking frying pan.

At first, it was just a mewing sound, tiny, soft, like a baby crying. Then it was something more. A rush of sound, a patter of paws. A bark. A meow. A howl.

"Uh-oh," Jordan said. "Trouble."

"Cow bone!" Terry said.

Jordan nodded and raced for the kitchen.

Terry raced for the porch.

Too late. Trouble was already streaking across the street.

# Chapter
# 3

Trouble was definitely streaking across the street to the Dunhill house, the perfect Dunhill house.

Inside, Mary Beth Dunhill was whirling around the kitchen, packing three lunches, eating her breakfast, and stuffing her backpack with the things for her day's work at the University Ocean Complex—charts, her photographs of dolphins, her notebooks.

Judith and Nora, her daughters, were sitting at the table, eating breakfast and watching. They exchanged looks and shrugged.

They knew better than to say anything when their mom was in one of these superefficient moods. Not that she wasn't always efficient: laboratory, research, dolphins, work. Work. More work. But sometimes, like now, she was incredible. Best to just stay out of her way.

Suddenly, as if Mary Beth were reading her daughters' minds, she stopped. Turned to the girls.

"And you two are to stay at the enrichment program *all* day today," she said, pointing a finger first at one, then the other. "At twelve and fourteen years old, you can't be out wandering the streets. Am I understood?"

Judith grinned. "You-are-understood-Mother," she said. She made her voice come out like a robot's.

"Ditto," Nora said.

Mary Beth frowned. "I mean it," she said. "I'm not in the mood for any more calls from the principal telling me that you've— What—"

All three of them turned at the sound of glass shattering somewhere—followed by something. Something that came streaking through the kitchen.

Mary Beth backed up against the counter. "What!" she said. "What was that?"

"Mrs. Rice's cat," Judith said calmly.

"Yup," Nora added. She grinned, pointing. "And that's a dog," she said.

It *was* a dog. Zeus. Zeus, streaking through, hot on the tail of the cat.

Both cat and dog raced once around the kitchen, then turned and circled back and disappeared in the direction from which they'd come.

"I know that dog," Judith said, looking at her sister. "It's Zeus. He belongs to the new people across the street."

"I don't believe it!" Mary Beth said. "This is lovely! Just lovely."

She grabbed her backpack, then ran toward the front, where the cat and dog had disappeared.

Her eyes widened as she surveyed the mess in the front room. A vase. Her favorite vase! Smashed. Glass everywhere. The dog and cat must have come in through the window. Right through the open window!

But where were they now? She looked around, out the window.

Crossing the street, coming toward her, was the new neighbor, Terry something-or-other. He was carrying some ridiculous-looking thing, a bone it looked like, a bone as big as a dinosaur bone.

He looked disheveled and worried, and he was muttering to himself. Well, if the girls were right and the dog belonged to him, he'd better be worried!

Mary Beth started for the door just as the cat raced past her again, almost knocking her over.

It leaped out through the window, and Zeus leaped after it, both of them landing in her flower garden. Her flower and rose garden!

"Get out of there!" Mary Beth yelled through the window.

She raced for the front porch, down the steps to her garden, following a trail of broken flower pots and broken flowers. In the garden, she just stopped and stared, feeling tears come to her eyes. Her flowers! Her beautiful flowers. Smashed.

Then she saw the dog and cat—the cat who was hiding behind a bush and the dog who had grabbed a garden hose and was shaking it furiously in his mouth, as if he thought he had the cat by the tail.

"Get out!" Mary Beth yelled.

"Stop!" Terry yelled, too.

But Zeus continued to shake the hose and to paw at the flowers.

"Get!" Mary Beth yelled again. "Get out of here!" She waved an arm at them.

Just then the cat leaped out of the bushes, right in front of her. It didn't turn and run for home. Instead, it went streaking into her rose garden. The dog streaked right behind, crushing more flowers and plants and vines as he went.

Mary Beth lunged for Zeus. She missed, tripped, and fell face first into the mess of the garden. Her backpack went flying, scattering books and papers and pictures to the wind.

Terry was right beside her by then, waving the huge cow bone.

"Zeus!" he yelled. "Zeus. Stop!"

Zeus saw the bone. He stopped.

Terry tossed the bone to him.

Zeus took one last look behind him. Then he took the bone in his mouth and settled down with it between his front paws, totally ignoring the cat.

Terry stepped around Zeus and cautiously approached Mary Beth.

"I'm sorry," he said, reaching out a hand to her. "Really. Let me help."

Mary Beth ignored his hand and scrambled to her feet, her face streaked with dirt and mud. "And just how do you propose to do that?" she asked, her voice shaking with anger.

Terry looked sheepishly at the broken flowers, crushed and torn up, lying every which way. He dropped to his hands and knees. "Well, like this," he said. He looked up at her. "Here. See, first we get these flowers back in the ground."

He began sticking plants into the earth.

Mary Beth made a huge, huffy breath through her

nose, then knelt beside him. She wiped an arm across her muddy face, snatched the flower from his hand. She planted it firmly in the ground, patting the dirt around it. "I have a very particular way of doing this," she said, speaking through her teeth. "Call me eccentric, but I like to put the roots *in* the ground. You know?"

Terry blushed, looked away. "Right," he said. He looked at another flower, also crushed. Gingerly, he picked it up. "This is an unfamiliar species to me," he said.

Mary Beth sat back on her heels, her hands on her knees, and stared at him. "Really," she said. She snatched that flower from him, too. "It's a rose," she said. "Well, it *was* a rose."

Terry looked down at his hands, then up at her. "'A rose by any other name,'" he said.

For just a moment, it looked as if she would smile, but then she turned away as she heard a whimper behind her.

Zeus. That creep! That miserable dog!

He had abandoned his bone and now had one of her pictures, her dolphin pictures that had fallen out of her backpack, firmly in his mouth.

"Give that to me!" she said. She held out her hand.

Zeus came quietly to her side and let her take the picture. Then, as though he was going to clean them all up for her, he went back to the scattered pictures and picked up another dolphin picture. He trotted back to her, his tail wagging.

"See," Terry said. "Zeus is sorry."

Mary Beth just rolled her eyes.

"Uh," Terry said. "We're, uh, new here."

13

Mary Beth looked down at her backpack and began stuffing pictures and things back into it. "Just renting for the week?" she said, her voice sarcastic—and hopeful.

"No," Terry said. "Actually, we're here till the end of July."

"Fabulous," Mary Beth said, that sarcastic sound still in her voice.

"I'm Terry Barnett," Terry said.

Mary Beth looked at him. She sighed. Well, she couldn't actually ignore the introduction.

"Mary Beth Dunhill," she said.

She nodded to the porch where Judith and Nora were standing—had been the whole time. Standing, watching, and smiling. Although when they saw their mom turn to them, they tried hard to look serious. "And those are my daughters," Mary Beth added. "Judith and Nora."

Judith muttered to her sister. "Maybe it's just me," she said, "but I think there's a visceral animal attraction between the two of them."

Nora nodded. "Yeah," she agreed. "Like Godzilla and Mothra."

They both made little waving signals with their hands to Terry.

He smiled, waved, and turned back to Mary Beth.

"Well," Mary Beth said. "I'd love to stay here in muddy, wet clothing and continue to exchange banal pleasantries, but I'm late for work and my daughters are late for summer school. So if you'll kindly take that"—she gestured toward Zeus—"that mutt out of my yard and go—"

"But what about your plants?" Terry said, all worried looking.

Mary Beth shrugged. "They've survived hurricanes. They can survive this." She made a motion to him. "Okay, now," she said. "Out."

Terry stood up, took a few backward steps. "Could I make it up to you? I mean, at least . . . do your laundry? Or something?"

Mary Beth shook her head, unbelieving. She stared down at his pants, at his muddy knees, at his messy shirt that looked as if he had slept in it. "Why don't you start with your own laundry?" she said sweetly.

Terry smiled—tried to smile. But then he just shrugged. "Come on, Zeus," he said softly. "I think we've overstayed our welcome."

But Zeus wasn't ready to go yet. He was carrying one more dolphin photo to Mary Beth.

She snatched it from his mouth, then turned to the porch and started up.

Behind her, Terry grabbed Zeus by the collar, pulling him away from the bushes where the cat was still hiding. "No, Zeus," he said. "No more."

Up on the porch, Mary Beth looked at her daughters. "Thanks for all your help," she said.

Judith and Nora looked down, trying to look apologetic.

"And what were you two smiling at before?" Mary Beth said.

"Us?" Judith said. She blinked. "Nothing, Mom. Really."

"Really, Mom," Nora said.

Mary Beth made the huffy sound again and slammed into the house.

Behind her, the girls grinned at one another. Then Nora pointed.

Across the street, where Terry was retreating, holding Zeus firmly by the collar, was Jordan. He was in the window, leaning out—had been the whole time—and was even now furiously snapping pictures of the whole mess.

Both girls silently gave him two thumbs up.

# Chapter
# 4

It took forever—seemed to, anyway—but finally the mess was cleaned up. Mary Beth was showered and ready for work, and the girls were off to summer school.

With her backpack again firmly on her back, Mary Beth pedaled off on her bike to the University Ocean Complex. The pictures of dolphins were still sticking out every which way, but her notebooks were, for the most part, back in some kind of order. Muddy order.

But now she was late. Good and late.

She pedaled hard, shaking her head. How could one small cat and a miserable mutt of a dog cause so much trouble? She'd have to have a talk with that new neighbor, that Terry person, and tell him to keep that mutt chained up.

Mary Beth slowed a bit, trying to calm herself. She couldn't remember when she'd been so angry, except maybe at Claude, that creep from work.

She heard a sound then, a woofy, whimpery sound, and she turned. Something behind her? Something following her?

She wobbled a bit on the bike, trying to look behind her.

Nothing.

Nothing she could see, anyway. Because Zeus cleverly stayed out of sight. He had slipped his chain and was happily following her. Actually, he was following the dolphin pictures that were still sticking out of her backpack.

Mary Beth turned back. She was imagining things, that's all, reacting to that miserable cat and miserable mutt on this miserable morning.

She pedaled more quickly again, trying to get her thoughts in order. What a rotten way to start a day— late. She was never late. What would happen to her dolphin? Roxanne was so special—special and fragile, too. Roxanne used to live in a tank, a Navy tank for experiments. Then they'd put her back in the ocean, and now Roxanne was afraid, afraid to have anything to do with any other dolphins. She'd become a real loner. Mary Beth was trying to reintroduce her to the other dolphins. Although, she had to admit to herself, it didn't seem to be working very well. Roxanne didn't trust. And now that Mary Beth was late, she'd maybe lose more of Roxanne's trust.

Mary Beth sighed. Well, dolphins must have neighbors, too, right? Maybe Roxanne would understand.

She got to the dock, dropped her bike against the hut, then hurried down into her tiny office, making her way through the maze of marine equipment that was everywhere.

Becky, her assistant, was already in the office, going through the mail.

"You're late!" she said, looking up. "Really late. I've been frantic. What happened?"

Mary Beth dropped her backpack. "Don't ask," she said.

"Tell that to Roxanne," Becky said, squinting up at Mary Beth. "You've never been late before. What if she's not there?" Becky threw the letters down on the table. "What if we never see her again? What if—"

Mary Beth put up a hand. "Somehow I don't think Roxanne is as neurotic a dolphin as you are a human. Now—"

Becky crossed her arms.

Mary Beth closed her eyes and took a deep breath. "I'm sorry, Becky," she said softly. "I am. I had a rough morning."

Becky nodded. "That's okay," she said. She looked down at the mail and picked up some envelopes. "I'm afraid it's about to get rougher, though," she said softly. "I'm sorry, but you've been rejected by the Christopher Foundation and the Mannheim. *And* the Delphi."

Mary Beth leaned back against a wall. "Great!" she said, pressing both hands against her head. "That leaves just the Rockland Marine Mammal grant. And if I don't get that I'll be . . ." She rubbed a hand across her face, closed her eyes a moment.

"Stocking goldfish at the local pet store," a voice said.

Mary Beth opened her eyes, looked up, and saw Claude Carver standing in the doorway, looking at her. Pompous. Slick. Overdressed. As usual.

Claude, who thought he knew everything. Who got his own way most of the time, even though he knew

19

practically nothing about dolphins—nothing decent and humane, anyway.

"Very humorous, Claude," she said. "Oh, wait a second, I forgot to laugh."

Claude moved into the room and came to stand beside her—too close beside her. As always.

As always, Mary Beth backed away from him.

"I wasn't joking, you know," he said. "Perhaps we should strive for that Rockland grant together? You know, the sum of the parts being greater than the whole and all that sort of thing? Hmmm?"

Mary Beth rolled her eyes. "No thanks," she said. "Our philosophies of marine study are too different."

"Really?" Claude said. He turned and smiled at Becky. "I didn't know I even had one," he said with a shrug.

"Figures," Mary Beth muttered.

Claude turned then and moved toward the door. "Let me know if you change your mind," he said.

As he left, Mary Beth made a face at his back.

Becky nodded. "I know," she said. "He should be studying sharks. He'd feel more at home."

"Yeah," Mary Beth said. "But if I don't get major funding soon, Roxanne is going to end up in a pen, doing sound recognition tests for the rest of her life. And probably for him!"

Becky nodded, sighed.

"Well, let's go," Mary Beth said.

She and Becky went upstairs to the dock and to the *Daily Planet,* the old lobster boat that was their research lab. Mary Beth was carrying a tape deck with her recordings of dolphin sounds, and Becky had the other materials for the day. Mary Beth's plans were to go out in the bay, circle a while, and try to call Roxanne from the depths. Try to coax her, lead her to join the other dolphins.

Up on the dock and around the corner, Zeus sat patiently waiting, his tail making little circles on the wooden planks.

He watched Mary Beth and Becky climb into their boat.

When they did, he stood up and approached slowly, his tail going.

Mary Beth was smiling slightly now. Just the thought of seeing Roxanne always made her feel easier. Roxanne was worth it, worth all the time, the effort. If only she'd come to them even though they were so late.

Mary Beth settled herself in the boat and put on her life vest as Becky went to work starting the engine. Mary Beth fiddled with her tapes a minute until small sounds came out—blats, whistles, clicks.

Dolphin sounds.

Mary Beth turned up the volume.

Zeus's ears went up.

Dolphins!

On the boat, Mary Beth leaned forward, studied the screens of the radar scanners.

Becky did, too. "So we play the voices of the other dolphins for Roxanne?" she said softly.

Mary Beth nodded.

"I wonder if we play them really softly, if she'll run away?" Becky said.

"I wonder about that, too." Mary Beth answered. She leaned toward the screen again. "Where are you, Roxanne?" she said. "I'm sorry I was late. Really. Will you forgive me?"

21

Nothing for a moment.

And then a little bleeping dot appeared on the screen.

Becky smiled. "That's her frequency," she said. "That good old Navy transponder just keeps on ticking inside her."

Mary Beth tapped the bleeping dot on the screen. "Good morning, Roxanne," she said. "Big day for you. We're going to introduce you to a nice pod of dolphins." She made a little frowny face at the screen. "You know, too much loneliness is a bad thing," she said.

She turned some controls to adjust the screen.

Becky put some pictures of dolphins on the table by Mary Beth, then turned away and prepared to launch the boat out into the bay. Mary Beth adjusted the dolphin sounds up, then lower, then up again.

Just then Zeus leaped from the dock onto the boat. Practically into Mary Beth's lap.

She backed up. "You!" she yelled.

"Oh, look!" Becky said. "Where'd he come from? He's adorable!"

"He is *not* adorable!" Mary Beth shouted.

"You're overreacting," Becky said. "Look at him. He's so cute."

As if to prove how cute he was, Zeus got up on his hind legs, looking at the dolphin pictures and whimpering.

"I'm not overreacting!" Mary Beth said. "If anything, I'm *under*reacting. You don't know. He's the one that made me late."

Zeus whimpered, looked from Mary Beth to the dolphin pictures, and whimpered again.

Mary Beth glared at Zeus. "We are not friends," she

said. She pointed a finger at him. "Now, get out of here. Go."

Zeus just looked up at her, whimpering faintly again. He didn't budge, though.

Mary Beth took a deep breath. She stood up, bent, scooped Zeus into her arms. Then she stepped off the boat and planted Zeus securely on the dock. "That's it, Zeus," she said. "Good-bye!"

She climbed back on the boat. "Done!" she said.

Becky was watching, smiling. When Zeus was gone, she just shrugged and started up the boat.

Slowly, it picked up speed, inching out into the bay.

Back on the dock, Zeus frantically watched it pull away. The boat that was going out to the dolphins. *His* dolphin!

He tore down the dock, yapping wildly. The boat had accelerated and was now too far away to reach. Lots of other boats were going out. But his was gone.

He looked this way. That way. Nothing.

Then he saw a way. A boat, a huge boat, big and fancy and fast. With Claude at the controls, it was just about to clear the other side of the dock, just starting out into the bay.

Zeus jumped and landed safely, right in the back of Claude's fancy boat.

The boat leaped forward in the water, racing until it was just alongside Mary Beth's boat. Then, before Claude could react, before Claude even saw him, Zeus leaped again. Right into the back of the boat that carried Mary Beth and Becky and the dolphin pictures. Into the boat that was going to look for dolphins.

# Chapter
# 5

For the first few minutes, neither Mary Beth nor Becky had any idea that there was a new passenger aboard. Mary Beth had come up to the bridge and was at the wheel, staring intently out over the water. Behind her, Becky was carefully setting up the sonar equipment, video cameras, notebooks, and charts, making a mini laboratory space on the table nearby. She also set out a bucket of fish for Roxanne, just in case the dolphin came close enough.

Zeus settled down behind them, his tail going in little circles again.

Suddenly, Becky leaned toward the radar screen, smiling. "Roxanne's in range now," she said softly.

Zeus cocked his head.

"You sure?" Mary Beth said.

Becky nodded. "Sure."

Zeus's ears came up.

"Great!" Mary Beth breathed. She shut down the engine.

A vast, sudden quiet settled over the water.

They sat there a moment, the boat rocking gently. Then slowly, carefully, Mary Beth dropped a hydrophone into the water to pick up sounds—dolphin sounds.

Immediately, she was rewarded. *Blat. Squawk.*

"There she is!" Becky whispered.

And she was. Like a miracle, Roxanne appeared, about a quarter mile out, leaping vertically from the water, twisting in the air like a figure skater, then plunging back into the blue water.

Again, she did it. Leaped. Twisted. Again and again.

Then she homed straight in on them, seeming to fly toward them, skimming the water, then diving under.

Then she was gone.

Becky and Mary Beth looked out over the water, hands shading their eyes from the sun. Nothing. A trail of bubbles was all that remained.

For a long moment, all was still. Just the bay. The silence. The sun on the water. The boat rocking gently.

*Pop! Squawk!*

Behind them!

They turned, laughing. Roxanne was behind them. She had swum under the boat and surfaced on the other side.

Mary Beth leaned over the side of the boat toward the dolphin, so close that she and Roxanne were almost eye to eye. Mary Beth could see the beauty of her markings, even see an old scar on her forehead.

*Pop! Blat!*

Roxanne made playful sounds, looking straight at Mary Beth.

"And good morning to you, too, Roxanne," Mary Beth said, laughing.

Roxanne turned on her back, flapped her tail once, hard, on the water, apparently waving hello.

It was more than Zeus could bear. He had been as quiet as he could for as long as he could.

He leaped up, racing up and down the deck in frantic excitement, barking.

"No, I don't believe it!" Mary Beth yelled. "I'm cursed. I am."

Becky bent, reached for Zeus as he raced past her, grabbed him, and pulled him to her.

"Hold on!" she said. She patted him. "Nice doggie," she said, trying to calm him. "Nice doggie."

"He is not a nice doggie!" Mary Beth said, her teeth gritted tight.

She turned and took a quick look at Roxanne.

Yes. She was still there.

Mary Beth turned back, glared at Zeus. "Stay out of our way," she said softly, pointing a finger at him. "I mean it. Stay out of our way or you get a free swimming lesson."

Zeus struggled against Becky's arms. He turned and eyed Roxanne, so close now that he, too, could look right in her eyes.

Roxanne looked back.

Zeus couldn't help it. He was overcome with joy. He wriggled free, leaped from Becky's arms, barked joyfully right in Roxanne's face.

But Roxanne didn't return his joy.

She turned. Dove under water. Disappeared. And didn't resurface.

For long minutes they waited. Nothing. She was gone.

Mary Beth leaned back against the rail, her hands pressed against her forehead. "Thanks a lot!" she said to Zeus. "Thanks. It's hard enough to even get near Roxanne without you totally freaking her out!"

Zeus backed away, lowered his tail. He sat quietly, head down.

He hadn't meant to scare Roxanne. He didn't want them mad at him.

But they were. Mary Beth was. Good and mad.

She stood up. Then, with a motion of her head to Becky, she climbed over the rail and lowered herself into the water. Then she, too, disappeared.

For a long minute, Becky and Zeus stayed on deck, scanning the water.

Nothing. No Mary Beth. No Roxanne. Nothing out there on the water. Nothing at all.

Becky got up and went below to the lower part of the boat, Zeus following.

A window. An observation window.

Becky was peering out, and Zeus came up alongside, peered out with her. It was dark out there, dark water, clear, dark water.

He whimpered and pressed his nose to the glass.

Suddenly, filling the window, looking in at him— Roxanne. The dolphin. *His* dolphin.

Wide-eyed, for a long moment, each stared at the other.

Zeus's heart was pounding wildly with joy, and he began to bark frantically.

Roxanne made a face, moved backward. In a moment, she had disappeared again.

All that was left was water. Dark, lonely, empty water.

Then Mary Beth swam into view. She glared in at Zeus, who set up a howl.

Becky picked him up and carried him up to the deck, just as Mary Beth was climbing back aboard the boat, shaking off water.

Becky reached for some crackers on the table behind her. Then she bent and put Zeus down carefully. "Maybe if we give him food, he'll calm down," she said.

"Maybe if he *becomes* food," Mary Beth said. "Maybe then he'll calm down."

Becky patted Zeus, then put a pan of water down in front of him. She rubbed his ears. "She didn't mean that," she said softly.

"I did, too," Mary Beth said. She bent, picked up the bucket of fish for Roxanne, and placed it at the open stern railing. "If only Roxanne would come back," she said. "She was so close. So close."

Then, like a miracle, Roxanne did appear. Her head popped out, right beside the boat, right beside Zeus. She lolled there, watching Zeus lapping up water.

Zeus lifted his head. Saw Roxanne watching him.

Then he did it again—leaped up, barking excitedly.

Roxanne didn't turn and dive this time, but she did make a face. Then she spit at him. A big stream of water, right in his face.

Zeus backed up. Then he lifted his leg and aimed a stream of water back. Right at her face.

Roxanne was fast, though. Fast and smart.

She leaped from the water, avoided the shower, and

dove back in. Performing a very strong tail slap, she sent a major splash, a wave, right onto Zeus.

Zeus howled. Yelped. Shook himself. And Roxanne disappeared under the water.

Zeus watched her go. Watched something else, too. Far out in the water, more dolphins, a whole bunch of dolphins.

Zeus's ears pricked up.

"Look!" Becky said, pointing where Zeus was looking.

Mary Beth nodded. "And look here," she said. She pointed to the radar screen.

For a long moment she and Becky stared fixedly at the screen, watching the radar blip that was Roxanne moving ever so slowly toward the many other blinking dots that were her family. A dolphin family that she never went near anymore.

"There's your family, Roxanne," Mary Beth said softly. "Go to them. Go on, Roxanne. They're not going to hurt you."

All three aboard the boat watched—Mary Beth, Becky, Zeus. Watched and waited.

The blinking dot on the screen continued on toward the others. Slowed. Slowed. Then stopped.

"Why?" Becky murmured quietly. "Why doesn't she trust?"

"I don't know," Mary Beth answered, still staring at the screen. "I think maybe it has something to do with Claude, her time with him. Something bad happened. Until something good happens, she's not going to trust again."

From out on the water, the dolphin sounds became

louder—blats, squawks, playful sounds from the other dolphins, as if they were calling to Roxanne.

But the dot on the screen still didn't move.

"Go on," Mary Beth urged again. "Go on, Roxanne. They're okay. They're family."

But Roxanne didn't seem to want a family. Her dot stayed just where it was.

"Please," Mary Beth whispered. "I may not be around here to feed you forever."

Still nothing. And worse, it suddenly became clear that Roxanne was fleeing. She surfaced, then dove, and disappeared from sight. She disappeared from the radar, from the other dolphins.

Nothing.

Mary Beth and Becky looked at one another. "Again," Becky said, sighing. "Maybe her karma is to always be solo."

Mary Beth sighed, too. "I know the feeling," she said.

They sat for just another minute, quietly. Then Mary Beth lifted anchor, and Becky started the engine. The boat headed back to shore.

Sadly, Zeus moved to the stern of the boat, looking behind, watching, hoping Roxanne would surface again. But there was nothing. Out behind them was nothing but waves, huge waves, as the boat moved away fast. Faster and faster it went, as if Becky or Mary Beth were using up all the pent-up anger and energy from the morning.

Fast it went. Then it hit a cross wave hard, and tumbled Zeus straight into the water.

# Chapter
# 6

Becky was yelling.

"Cut!" she yelled. "Cut the engines. Zeus!"

Suddenly, the engines were stilled and silence filled the bay.

"What?" Mary Beth yelled back.

"Zeus!" Becky said. "He's gone."

"No," Mary Beth said.

"Yes," Becky said.

Mary Beth turned, looked out over the water, then slumped, putting her hands to her head. "Great!" she said. "This is just great. My new neighbor's going to think I did this on purpose. I shanghaied his dog and fed him to the sharks." She smiled slightly at Becky and raised her eyebrows. "Not that I wasn't considering it."

"You were not," Becky said.

"Okay, I wasn't," Mary Beth said.

They both scanned the bay then, their eyes squinted

31

against the glare of the sun. Nothing. Nothing but water. And a wave where the boat had cut through the water.

Mary Beth leaned over the railing. "Zeus!" she called softly. "Zeus, are you out there? Come on. This is no longer amusing."

As if Zeus didn't know that.

He was paddling, struggling frantically. Swim. Swim! But how?

His little paws paddled madly. He bobbed up to the surface. He barked. He barked again. Paddled harder. Stop! Come back. Nothing. The boat was far away.

Scary. It was scary out there. Black water all around. His heart was thumping wildly. He was alone, alone out there.

Alone, but for whatever was under the water. Under and coming toward him. Something huge. Something powerful.

Something scary.

He yapped again, frantically. Come get me, come back!

Nothing. Just that presence under the water.

A shark. Under water, a shark was racing toward him, and Zeus knew instantly that whatever it was, it was bad. Dead bad.

Zeus struggled, trying to keep his head above the surface. He wasn't even even barking anymore. He was too tired. Needed his breath.

The creature was close now, scary close, closing in on him.

Close enough that when it suddenly surfaced, Zeus could see teeth. Huge teeth. In huge jaws.

Then it dove again. Not away from him but down under him. And it was coming up at him. Right at him.

Then Zeus saw something else. Far out in the water—too far?—a dolphin. Heading toward him. Roxanne?

She skimmed the water, not even breaking a wave, skimming toward him almost on top of the water.

The shark moved up beneath Zeus, so close, Zeus could feel its rough back—or was that teeth?

But Roxanne was on the way. Racing. Closing the distance between them. Speeding to him.

Yes. She reached him. Dove under, surfaced.

The shark surfaced, too, its ferocious teeth gleaming in its ferocious jaw. Face-to-face. Dolphin and shark.

Roxanne moved in on the shark, making fierce popping sounds. *Blat! Squawk. Pop!*

The shark moved toward Roxanne, its huge black head glistening in the sun.

Roxanne's sounds became wilder. *Blat! Pop. Crack. Whistle.*

The shark opened its jaws, teeth gleaming.

Suddenly, Roxanne flew forward and butted heads with the shark. She was so huge, so powerful, that the shark was forced backward, forced to retreat. But only for a moment. It swam away, then turned, circled lazily, and headed back, swimming relentlessly toward Zeus.

Roxanne dove under, turned, surfaced. Again headed back. Again she butted her head against the shark, butted so hard, so forcibly this time, that the shark was not just forced, but almost flung backward, actually spinning in the water.

Roxanne dove again.

This time though, it seemed the shark had had enough. It dove. Disappeared. And didn't reappear.

Only Roxanne and Zeus were left bobbing in the water.

Roxanne dove again, under Zeus. When she surfaced, Zeus was on her back. Safe on her back.

Zeus barked. Licked Roxanne's neck. Barked again. Safe! He was safe.

Roxanne headed straight for the boat, where Mary Beth and Becky were still frantically searching the water for any sign of the missing Zeus.

That's when Becky pointed. "Oh, my gosh!" she whispered.

"What?" Mary Beth said.

Becky pointed again.

Mary Beth turned.

Zeus. Zeus riding Roxanne, riding the waves, joyously, as though they were the star attraction at Sea World.

Becky stared for just a minute. Then she snatched at the video camera on the table beside her and started it rolling.

For a full minute, Becky recorded them swimming strong, straight toward the boat. When they came right alongside, Mary Beth scrambled down the ladder on the side.

As soon as Roxanne was in close enough, Mary Beth reached out, grabbed Zeus, and gently lifted him back to safety.

She climbed back on deck, Zeus in her arms, and set him down. "Are you okay?" she said.

He shook himself, drenching her.

"You're fine," she muttered.

Beside them, Roxanne leaned her head against the boat, looking straight at Zeus.

Zeus looked back, barking happily.

Then Roxanne made a sound, a new sound, unlike

anything she'd done before. A sound like a bark. As if she was imitating Zeus, or trying to.

Zeus screwed up his face and made a sound at Roxanne—something like a whistle, like one of her sounds. But it came out a bit like a sigh or a tiny howl.

"They're talking to each other," Mary Beth whispered. "They're talking to each other!"

"They've bonded," Becky whispered.

"This is incredible," Mary Beth whispered back. "Keep rolling. I can't believe it. I just can't believe it."

She grabbed the tape recorder, clicked it on, holding her breath, her heart racing.

As if to oblige, Roxanne and Zeus continued talking to one another. They got louder and louder—whistles, barks, blats—each seeming to try to outdo the other.

Then—maybe she had said good-bye—Roxanne dove under the water and was gone.

The whole bay was suddenly still.

Mary Beth took a deep breath, put the recorder down, and turned to Becky. "Do you realize the ramifications of this?" she asked, laughing, her eyes wide. "Do you realize what this means? Do you?"

Becky put down the camera. "Not totally," she said, breathing hard. "But I know one thing for sure: You're going to get that Rockland grant."

Mary Beth threw back her head, laughed with pure joy. Then she turned and scooped Zeus up in her arms. "I love this dog!" she said. She buried her face in his fur. "Always did. From the minute I met him."

Zeus knew that.

He happily, sloppily, kissed her back.

35

# Chapter
# 7

As the little boat with Zeus aboard sped back toward the harbor, Claude was strutting around inside the center, ordering people around. Ordering the dolphins around, too. He strode up and down between the dolphin pens, his shiny briefcase in his hand, pointing first at this pen, then at that one, barking out orders.

His assistants, Linda and Phil, followed him, sending occasional secret looks to each other, as if they wished they could feed him to the sharks.

Claude stopped outside a pen and gestured to Phil. "That one!" he said, nodding toward the tank. "Work on him."

Phil's eyes opened wide. "Are you sure, Dr. Carver?" he asked, frowning. "Alex here is just coming off three straight days of the Greek alphabet and—"

Claude raised a finger, interrupting him. "Yes, I'm sure," he said. "Resume with number thirty-four U."

Phil sighed, made a note on his pad, then flipped

through a pile of plastic flash cards, looking for the proper one to begin the dolphin's work.

"And push this series to the limit," Claude continued. "Sixteen twenty-minute shifts interspersed with five-minute rest periods."

Phil looked up and started to protest, but Claude was already striding toward the next pen.

Phil followed, his mouth a tight line.

Claude stopped outside another pen, one where a mother and baby dolphin were cavorting playfully. "That one!" he said, pointing. "Put the mother in Tank Six. Separate her and the baby."

Phil and Linda exchanged looks again.

For a moment, neither moved. Then, reluctantly, Linda stepped forward. Without a word, she slid open a barrier between the two tanks. Using some food, she coaxed the mother into the next tank. When the mother dolphin was away from the baby, Linda shut the gate, separating mother and baby.

Linda took a deep breath, then closed her eyes a moment. She knew what would happen next, how the mother would react.

It took just a moment. And then it happened. Behind her, the mother dolphin suddenly realized the trick. She began making sounds, sad, worried, clicking sounds to her child, frantically looking over at the next tank, toward her baby.

Linda bit her lip, looked at Claude.

Nothing. His face was a mask. Bland. Cold. But smiling.

He leaned forward to the pen. "Now, now, mother," he said, shaking a finger at the mother dolphin. "This is no time for sentimentality. Your sacrifice is for the good of all mankind." He took a slow, deep breath. "And for science," he added virtuously.

Behind him, Phil leaned close to Linda. "And for Dr. Claude Carver," he muttered.

"All right. Now," Claude said. He turned and looked from Phil to Linda. "Begin the sonar recognition test series. Increase the volume of the masking sounds until the mother and child can no longer communicate through the wall." He turned away. "This way!" he said.

He gestured to the dock, pointing the way with his shiny briefcase.

When they came onto the dock, Mary Beth's boat was just chugging in to moor right beside Claude's boat—Claude's shiny research boat—where workers were putting in something else new and shiny: a docking platform for a mini-sub.

A shiny new mini-sub.

Claude put down his briefcase and stood smiling, arms folded, looking toward Mary Beth's boat. She would be impressed. She'd have to be.

She was. "Wow!" she said as soon as the engine of her boat subsided and she could be heard. She stared at the sub, wide-eyed. "Where'd you get that submersible?"

Claude smiled. "Pulled a few strings. You know." He raised his eyebrows. "Maybe one day you'd like to go down in it?"

"Yeah, I'd love to," Mary Beth said. "Solo."

She stepped from her boat onto the dock, Zeus right on her heels.

As soon as she was on the dock, Claude moved close to her, in the way he had of invading her space. "I keep telling you," he said, in a superpatient voice as though he were talking to a stubborn two-year-old. "Two keen scientific minds are better than one, Mary Beth."

"Yes," Mary Beth said. "But neither is any good without the missing ingredient."

She stepped back, putting distance between herself and Claude, then bent to pat Zeus. Funny. Zeus was a dog, but he had the missing ingredient, she was sure of it.

"Oh?" Claude said. He bent, too, and put out a hand to Zeus. "Nice doggie," he said.

Zeus growled, backing away.

Claude shrugged and stood up. "And what might that missing ingredient be?" he said.

"Heart," Mary Beth said, looking up at him. She patted Zeus again. "Just heart," she repeated softly.

She stood up then, looked at Claude, then looked over at the mini-sub. How she'd love to have that for her research!

"Speaking of heart," Claude said. "How goes your highly compassionate reintroduction study?"

It was sarcastic, the way he said it, but Mary Beth chose to ignore that. Instead, she looked at Zeus again. He was now gently nudging Claude's briefcase out of his way. Out of Claude's way, too. Out of anyone's way, in fact. It was well on its own way toward the water.

Mary Beth looked back at Claude, biting back a smile. "Roxanne is making some progress," she said.

"Well, good luck," Claude said. "I mean, you'll probably need it. Because I must say that I just don't think it's going to work."

He turned, then bent to pick up his briefcase just as Zeus gave it one last nudge and sent it tumbling into the water.

"You little mongrel!" Claude yelled.

He reached for Zeus. But Mary Beth was quicker. She bent and scooped Zeus protectively into her arms, backing up quickly.

"I'm going to drop-kick him from here to Miami!" Claude yelled.

"No you're not!" Mary Beth said. "Oh, no, you're not."

She hugged Zeus to her as Claude threw himself to the dock and reached in for the floating briefcase. Then Mary Beth scrambled from the dock to solid ground. It was time for her and Zeus to have lunch.

Mary Beth walked slowly back to town, walking the bike so Zeus could trot along at her side. She was heading for the hamburger stand for lunch, something she rarely did, since she mostly ate salads. But she decided that Zeus deserved a treat, a big, fat hamburger treat.

At the stand, a bunch of kids were hanging around, yelling and clapping about something.

Mary Beth made her way past them into the hamburger place. When she came out, she put a hamburger down on the sidewalk in front of Zeus.

"Here you go, Zeus," she said, rubbing his head, scratching at his ears. "I think you deserve this." She leaned her head against his for a moment. "Thank you," she whispered to him. "Thank you, thank you, thank you."

Zeus wagged his tail, then hunkered down and began happily scarfing down the hamburger.

Mary Beth smiled and stood up. She leaned against the building, eating her hamburger, letting the sun warm her, the emotions of the morning warming her, too.

What a morning! What an incredible morning! She'd surely get that grant now.

She looked down at Zeus again.

Communicating! Roxanne and Zeus had definitely been communicating!

She sighed, breathed in the calm of the summer day, then looked around her.

She could see the group of teens by the other side of the hamburger stand. They were in a big circle, surrounding some kids who were doing tricks on skates, yelling and clapping.

Scruffy-looking kids. Not like her own girls.

She smiled then. Good girls, they were, Judith and Nora, even though they worried her a lot. Always into something. And growing up! Goodness, how could they be growing so fast?

She straightened up and walked casually toward the teens, Zeus following. What were kids up to these days with these in-line skates? Breaking their necks, probably. That kind of skate hadn't even been invented when she was a kid. She stood on the edge of the circle, craning her neck to see.

Inside the circle, she could see the kids. Two of them. They were doing something incredible. Incredible and scary—spinning around and around, then leaping up and doing a full circle. And landing squarely on two feet. Most of the time. Some of the time they spun and fumbled, looking as if they were going to break their necks. Over and over, they did it. Amazing.

There were two of them performing. A boy and a girl.

She frowned. The girl? The girl was . . . She elbowed her way in to see better.

The boy . . . who was he?

41

And the girl. The girl was Judith.

Judith? Her Judith?

And on the sidelines, clapping ecstatically, was Nora.

Nora? Her Nora?

Nora and Judith? Her daughters? Who were supposed to be in summer school?

Mary Beth took a deep breath. She could feel the anger—no, the fear—rising in her throat.

Well, anger and fear.

Taking another deep breath, she pushed her way into the center of the circle. She raised her hand and pointed her finger at the girls.

"Busted!" she said.

# Chapter
# 8

"Uh-oh," Judith said.

"Uh-oh," Nora muttered.

Mary Beth jerked her thumb. "Now," she said.

Nora and Judith exchanged looks and shrugged.

Then they gave a last look at their friends and hurried after their mom.

Mary Beth was furious, so furious she was breathing hard, racing along, pushing her bike, not even waiting to see if the girls were following. Although they'd better be.

Behind her, Judith looked at Nora.

Nora looked back.

Judith raised her eyebrows.

Nora nodded.

Their private signal.

Both girls hurried to catch up with their mom. They knew how to get around her. Take the offensive. Always.

"So let me see if I have this straight," Judith said, ignoring the fact that her mom looked as if she were going to explode. "You don't want us to have *any* fun this summer, right?"

Mary Beth turned, her face an angry red. She stuck a finger in Judith's face. "What I want is this: I want you *not* hanging out with borderline juvenile delinquents performing daredevil skating stunts."

Judith tossed her head. "Craig is not borderline," she said.

Mary Beth shook her head, turned away. Then she took a deep breath and turned back. Quietly, puzzled, she said, "How'd you learn to skate like that anyway?"

"From me!" Nora said proudly.

Judith shot her sister a look. "Brilliant," she said.

Nora just shrugged.

"I suppose," Mary Beth said as they turned the corner to their house, "you two have been ditching your enrichment classes?"

"No!" Judith said. "We were just—"

"Rescheduling," Nora said.

Mary Beth started up the steps to the house, Zeus following happily. At the top step, Mary Beth turned and faced her girls. She pointed a finger first at one, then at the other. "Grounded," she said. "One week."

Judith sighed, looked down. Then she said, "Hey! Zeus. What's he doing with you?"

"Yeah," Nora said. "I thought you wanted him dead."

"Zeus!" someone yelled.

They all turned as Jordan came racing out of his house, tearing across the street to them, his dad right on his heels.

Jordan was holding a huge paper in his hand, like a photographic proof sheet. He dropped it on the porch and bent to hug Zeus.

"Zeus!" he said. "Zeus. Where have you been?"

"Good question," Nora muttered.

Zeus bounded into Jordan's lap as Jordan roughed him up, rubbing his ears, pressing his face into his neck.

"Where'd you guys find him?" Jordan said, looking up at them. "I've been looking all over for him. I even interrupted Dad's music."

"Yeah," Terry said. "But I told him Zeus would turn up. He always does. I told him Zeus was probably enjoying the sun somewhere."

Mary Beth seemed to blush. "Well," she said, "actually, he was. I mean, Zeus found me." She looked at Jordan, frowning. "Who are you?" she asked.

"Jordan Barnett," Jordan answered. He stood up and nodded toward his dad. "I'm with him. That's Terry."

Mary Beth smiled a small smile. "Yes," she said. "I know. We became acquainted this morning."

Terry bent then, patted Zeus, wiped some crumbs off his fur. "Looks like you became a little better acquainted with Zeus," he said. He smiled up at her. "In fact," he said, "I'd say you two look almost friendly."

Mary Beth shrugged. "Miracles sometimes happen."

Jordan bent to pick up the page of photographs.

"What's that?" Judith said, nodding at it.

"Oh," Jordan said. "I was just coming out of the darkroom when I saw Zeus." He held out the proof sheet.

Nora and Judith both looked at it.

Judith's eyes got wide, and Nora made a snorting sound, as if she was holding back a laugh. Only she didn't—hold it back, that is. She was suddenly convulsed with laughter.

"What?" Mary Beth said. "What's so funny?"

"Oh my gosh!" Judith yelped.

"Incredible!" Nora said. And she went into fresh fits of laughter.

"What's so funny?" Mary Beth said.

Jordan held the sheet toward her.

Mary Beth looked at it. Terry looked over her shoulder.

Pictures. Of Zeus tearing up flowers. Of Zeus shaking the hose. Of Mary Beth facedown in the mud. Covered with mud. Looking up at the camera, covered in mud.

Mary Beth handed the sheet back to Jordan. "Charming," she said.

Judith bit her lip, but she couldn't resist a comment. "Looking good, Mom," she said.

"Awesome," Nora added.

Mary Beth smiled sweetly at both girls. "Working on *two* weeks grounded, right?" she said.

Judith looked at Nora.

Nora looked back.

They both shrugged. Then both turned to Jordan.

"So," Judith said. "Your house has a satellite dish, doesn't it?"

"Yup," Jordan said. "Want to see all the channels we get?"

"Sure," Nora said. She turned. "Mom?" she said.

"Grounded," Mary Beth said. "Remember?"

"It's just across the street!" Judith said.

"And they're our neighbors!" Nora added.

Mary Beth thought a moment. They were her neighbors. And she did need the dog. And they owned the dog.

"Okay," she said, grudgingly. "But not *all* the channels. Right?"

"Right," Judith said.

The kids rushed across to Jordan's house, leaving Mary Beth and Terry standing there alone. Even Zeus had abandoned them and followed the kids.

They were both quiet a minute.

Finally, Mary Beth broke the silence. "Your dog was out on my boat all day," she said.

Terry made a face. "Sorry," he said. "I'll make sure it doesn't happen again."

"It's all right," Mary Beth said. "I mean, actually it seems to . . . well, agree with him."

Terry frowned at her. "Really?" he said.

"Really," Mary Beth said. "The wind through his hair—I mean, his fur. The—"

Terry nodded. "Right," he said. His voice took on a mocking tone. "The waves crashing against his canine face as he hoists the mizzen mast. Well, shiver me timbers and—"

"Now, stop!" Mary Beth said. "It's not that. It's—"

"Hey!" Terry said, holding up one hand. "You can take Zeus on a cruise to Antarctica if you want. Fine with me. Except he's Jordan's dog."

"Oh," Mary Beth said. "He is?"

Terry nodded. "He is."

"Oh," she said again. She nodded across the street to his house. "Then you'll excuse me? Can I talk to him?"

"Sure," Terry said. "Be my guest."

They both crossed the street to Terry's house. Inside, in the living room, the girls were huddled around the TV, fighting over the remote control.

"Where'd Jordan go?" Mary Beth asked, making her way into the room, stepping over piles of clothes,

47

records, tapes. There were sheets of music, pictures, a dog bone—stuff everywhere.

"Down there," Judith said, nodding toward the hall and holding the remote up so Nora couldn't reach it. "He's in his room with Zeus." She yelped at her sister, "Stop that!"

"Give it to me!" Nora said, tugging at Judith's arm.

Judith held the remote up, out of her sister's reach. "In a minute," she said. "I'll let you watch the Marlins game if you give me just fifteen minutes of music videos."

"Ten," Nora said.

"Hey!" Jordan called from his room. "Don't you guys have two TV's at home?"

"Us?" Judith called back. She continued to hold the remote out of Nora's reach. "This is going to sound really lame," she said. "We don't have even *one* TV in our house."

"Just call us a media-impaired family," Nora called.

"For good reason!" Mary Beth interjected. And then she added, "Jordan? Can I talk to you."

"Sure. In here," he called.

Mary Beth walked down the hall, stopped at the door to his room, and looked in.

Jordan was bent over, getting something from the table by the bed. Zeus was sitting on the bed, ears pricked up, watching her.

The room was incredible. Beautiful. Neat. Not at all like the living room. It was perfectly organized, with photos on the wall, incredibly beautiful photographs of all sorts of things.

"Wow!" Mary Beth said, looking from the pictures to Jordan. "Did you do these?"

Jordan nodded, smiling.

Mary Beth came farther into the room. She went over to one wall and studied the photos, leaning in to see the details: Zeus wearing sunglasses and standing on a surfboard, Zeus blindfolded before a firing squad made up of stuffed animals, Zeus and Terry and Jordan together. And a very beautiful photograph of a very beautiful woman, smiling directly into the camera.

"Wow!" Mary Beth said, turning to Jordan again. "You did all these?"

Jordan nodded.

Mary Beth moved slowly around the room, looking at the photos, one after the other. She stopped at the desk and picked up a collage of photos. "And this?" she said.

Jordan smiled and moved over to look at it with her. "That's going to be the cover for my dad's opera score," he said proudly.

Mary Beth looked at him, her eyes wide. "He—your dad—he's writing an opera?"

Jordan nodded. "A rock opera. Most of the time he does music for commercials and very tall elevators." He frowned at Mary Beth. "But that's only to pay the bills," he said.

"Hey!" Mary Beth said. "If his opera is anywhere near as good as your cover art, I'm sure it's excellent."

"Thanks," Jordan said. He paused a moment. "But Terry's blocked right now," he said sadly. "I think he's lost a melody."

He turned then, looked at a framed photo, the last one he'd ever taken of his mom.

Mary Beth looked where he was looking, at the beautiful woman she'd noticed before. "Is that your mom?" she said quietly.

49

"She died," Jordan said.

"I'm sorry," Mary Beth said. "I bet you miss her a lot."

Jordan looked away. "Yeah," he said. He swallowed. "We both do."

There was quiet for a minute, and then Mary Beth spoke. "Jordan?" she said tentatively. "I need to ask you something."

Jordan looked at her, a sheepish look on his face. "I know," he said. "You want me to clean up the mess my dad made this morning."

Mary Beth chewed on her lip. Not a bad idea. But she shook her head. "Never mind that," she said. "But see, I'm a marine biologist, and I'd like your permission to take Zeus out on my boat a few times to participate in an important research project."

"Zeus?" Jordan said. "How come Zeus?"

"Well," Mary Beth said, "I don't know how to say this, but I think he may be capable of . . . well, maybe he's talking. Interspecies communication, actually."

Jordan shrugged. "What's the big deal? I talk to Zeus all the time."

"It *is* a big deal," Mary Beth said. "Because I think Zeus was talking to my dolphin."

"You own a dolphin?" Jordan said, his eyes wide.

Mary Beth smiled. "Roxanne lives in the bay," she said. "But I kind of take care of her."

"Where'd you get her?" Jordan asked.

"From Claude Carver," Mary Beth said. "He's a— well, a researcher. He calls himself that, anyway. But the point is, she used to live in a tank, and we put her back in the ocean. Now, though, she won't have anything to do with other dolphins. But"—Mary Beth laughed—"but

50

for some reason, she seems to like Zeus. I mean, really like Zeus."

"Wow!" Jordan said.

"So," Mary Beth went on, "it would be really great if Zeus and Roxanne could, you know, kind of get together and—"

Jordan was frowning.

"What?" Mary Beth said.

Jordan shrugged. "I have to ask him. Zeus. See, it has to be his decision."

"Oh," Mary Beth said. Then she added, "Of course, you could come along, too. Zeus would like that. I mean, I'd like that. You could take the pictures. Record the event for posterity."

Jordan was just shaking his head. He turned to Zeus, who was sitting up straight on the bed, ears up, looking from one to the other and listening to the whole conversation.

"Zeus's decision," Jordan said again.

Mary Beth turned to Zeus, too.

Suddenly, in her head, she saw pictures of that morning on the boat, of her dumping Zeus out onto the dock. She heard in her mind some of the things she'd said about wanting Zeus to be shark food, about giving him a swimming lesson.

I didn't mean it, she told him, inside her head. I didn't.

Zeus looked back at her, thoughtfully, head cocked.

Really! she told him silently. It was just a joke.

Zeus blinked.

I bought you a hamburger, she told him. Don't forget that.

Suddenly, Zeus nodded. He jumped up. He wagged

his tail. He barked once. A joyful bark. The kind of bark he had barked at Roxanne.

Mary Beth smiled, took a deep breath.

Then Zeus leaped off the bed and trotted on down the hall, Jordan and Mary Beth following.

Thank you, Zeus, Mary Beth whispered inside her head, thank you, thank you, thank you.

In the living room, Nora and Judith turned quickly when their mom arrived. They were smiling, smug looking. They'd been up to something, but Mary Beth wasn't going to ask what, not for the moment.

"We're doing it, Dad," Jordan said. "Zeus and I, we're going out on the boat with Mary Beth."

Terry smiled. "Good for you!" he said.

Jordan nodded. "It is good," he said. He bent over, picked up Zeus, holding him tight. "Only thing is," he said hesitantly. "I wish I were a better swimmer. Like you."

"Huh?" Terry said. "You're a great swimmer! What are you talking about?"

Jordan shook his head. "Not in the ocean," he said. He bent his head over Zeus. "If only I had someone with me," he said softly. "Someone who could fish me out in case there was a terrible accident."

He peeked over Zeus, looking quickly at Nora and Judith.

They looked back, grinning.

Instantly, they'd figured out what he was up to. Well, why not? Maybe it'd help both parents to chill out. Besides, their parents were lonely. Anyone could see that.

"Don't worry about swimming or accidents," Mary

52

Beth said. "There's no problem with that. My assistant has lifeguard certification."

"Unh, huh," Judith said quickly, shaking her head hard. "Becky's too busy working the boat and equipment."

"Right," Nora said. "And so are you."

They all turned and looked at Terry.

Terry squinted at Jordan. He looked at the girls. He looked back at Jordan.

All three of them looked wide eyed and innocent.

He folded his arms. "Subtle," he said. "Very subtle. So you need me with you, right?"

"Right," Jordan said. His smile was purely angelic.

For just a minute, Terry kept on staring. But then he saw that Judith and Nora were smiling. Even Mary Beth was trying to bite back a smile.

He threw up his hands and smiled back.

# Chapter
# 9

By late the next afternoon, everything seemed different, happier, somehow. Mary Beth acted happier. The girls and Jordan seemed happy, too, in spite of the girls being grounded. And Terry definitely seemed happier, even humming a bit as he worked on his motorcycle in the driveway.

Zeus especially was relaxed and happy, lying in the sun, sleeping.

They had gone out on the boat that day, all but the girls, who were condemned to the enrichment program, and there was no doubt that Zeus and Roxanne had done some great bonding. They had talked and yapped and barked and whistled. It seemed each was learning the other's language, as well as the sign language Mary Beth was trying to teach Roxanne. Zeus and Roxanne had even played ball together, and Zeus had barked to Roxanne to go bring back fish. Jordan had photographed it all, dolphin and dog bonding and talking to each other.

So now, in the late afternoon, Terry sat on the pavement in his driveway, working on his motorcycle. Next to him, his boom box was softly playing a melody.

There was a sound, something that caused him to look up. Across the street, he saw Mary Beth come out on her porch and set down a flower pot. Terry watched her, watched the graceful way she bent, touched a flower gently before straightening up.

When she stood up, she turned, saw him looking. She smiled.

Terry smiled back.

For just a moment, each watched the other.

And then, slowly, wiping his hand on an old rag, Terry got to his feet.

Maybe . . .

Maybe what? He didn't know. But she was standing, watching him, smiling a little. Waiting.

For him?

He started across the street to her. But no sooner did he step off the curb than a car, a huge, four-wheel-drive vehicle, one of those yuppie things as big as a tank, came hurtling down the street, shuddering to a stop in front of Mary Beth's house.

"Hey!" Terry yelled, when the driver stopped. "Watch where you're going!"

The driver got out, turned, and eyed Terry. "I *was* looking," he said. He looked Terry up and down, his nose wrinkled as though something bad was in the air. "Was and am," he said.

"Yeah, well, you were driving too fast!" Terry answered, his face suddenly hot.

The driver turned from Terry, looked up at Mary Beth standing on the porch, then back at Terry.

"Sorry," he added. "I was rather in a hurry to visit Mrs. Dunhill. Apparently, so were you. And you failed to properly look both ways before crossing the street. Thank goodness for antilock brakes."

Terry was about to say something about antilock brains, but just then Mary Beth called out.

"Claude?" she said. She came down the steps and crossed to the curb. "What are you doing here?"

Claude bent into his car and pulled out a thick sheaf of books and papers from the front seat. He straightened up and turned to her. "Here," he said, holding out the pile. "These are the manuals for the submersible."

"For the sub? How come?" Mary Beth asked.

"Because it's yours!" Claude said, smiling. "Whenever you want it." His arms were still outstretched, the manuals held toward her.

Mary Beth backed up, squinting at him. "Really?" she said.

"Really," Claude said.

Mary Beth just stared at him, nodding slowly. "Why?" she said, at last.

Claude shrugged. "Why not?"

For a long minute, neither of them spoke.

Terry watched, looking from one to the other.

Mary Beth's look was hard. Suspicious.

Claude's face was blank, bland, as if he was trying to convey something but not succeeding. Sincerity, maybe.

After a moment, the hard look in Mary Beth's eyes began softening.

"You mean that?" she said.

Claude nodded. "I mean that," he said. "Invite me in? I'll go over the manuals with you."

Mary Beth stared at him for just another minute, making up her mind. Then she nodded toward the house. "Okay," she said. "Come on."

They both started up the steps to the house, when suddenly, Mary Beth turned back. "Uh, Terry?" she said. "Did you need something?"

Terry didn't answer for a long minute. "That's okay," he finally said softly. "Wasn't important."

Mary Beth turned away again, and she and Claude went into the house, Mary Beth leading the way to the kitchen, Claude following.

In the kitchen, Claude put the manuals on the table and rubbed his arms.

"Okay," Mary Beth said, turning to him. "What's the catch?"

Claude shrugged. "No catch," he said. "Really, Mary Beth. Why does there always have to be a— Whoa!" he yelled.

He threw out his arms as Nora came rolling into the kitchen on her skates, followed by Judith, both of them almost knocking him off his feet.

"Whoa!" Nora said. "Sorry!"

"Sorry, too," Judith said. She smiled at her mother. "We're going for a test ride," she said.

"Wait a minute," Mary Beth said, giving them each a stern look. "I believe you're grounded."

"Oh, Mom, just down the block," Nora said. "That's all."

"With Jordan and Zeus," Judith added. "Please?"

"Please?" Nora said.

57

Mary Beth looked at Claude, then back at the girls. Jordan. Zeus.

"Okay," she said slowly. She looked at her watch. "But just down the block. Right?"

"Right," Judith said. Both girls nodded agreement, Judith giving her mom a thumbs-up sign.

They rolled out the door as Claude turned back to Mary Beth. "Now, where were we?" he said.

"The catch?" Mary Beth said.

Claude spread his hands, all innocence. "No catch," he said.

Mary Beth gave him a long, cool look. With Claude, there was always a catch.

She sighed. Then looked down at the manuals. How she'd love that sub, that wonderful sub for her wonderful research. For Roxanne.

She looked up at Claude again.

If only she could believe him.

If only she could trust.

She had a funny moment then, thinking about Roxanne.

Maybe they could both learn to trust?

Then, as if he really meant it—had no other plans, no catch—Claude nodded to the manuals and started for the door.

"If you need help," he called over his shoulder, "just let me know."

Mary Beth smiled, this small feeling of joy and relief welling up inside her.

She walked with him out to the porch, down the steps, and out to the curb. All the while, she was trying to quell the feeling of excitement and at the same time, trying not to squash it, wanting to cherish it.

Could it be true? Was this sub really hers—no strings attached?

When they got to the curb, Claude leaned against the car, arms folded, a smile on his face.

"So," he said. "I'm hearing things about this dog. I'm to believe that cute little dog and your dolphin are actually talking?"

Mary Beth nodded, smiling widely. The pictures of Zeus and Roxanne flashed through her head: Zeus and Roxanne playing ball, Zeus barking, Roxanne clicking and trying to bark, Zeus whistling or trying to.

Mary Beth grinned up at Claude. "Incessantly," she said. "They're talking incessantly. I can hardly believe it. Zeus is even learning sign language. I've been showing him. And he's . . . well, it's hard to describe. But he told Roxanne to go get fish, and Roxanne actually did it, brought the fish back and dumped them on the deck."

Claude pushed out his lips, shoved his hands deep in his pockets, and rocked back and forth on his heels. "You know," he said. "I've got all the language skills data on file. Perhaps you might want to reconsider pooling our research? We could apply for the grant together, you know."

For one long minute, Mary Beth stared at him.

The catch! There it was—the catch.

Slowly, she shook her head. "The Rockland Marine Mammal grant?" she said softly. "I see. The catch. Sorry, Claude. But no. I've already applied for my grant."

She smiled at him again, a bittersweet smile. "But thanks anyway. And thanks for sharing your mini-sub. It was so unselfish of you."

She turned then and went back up the steps. At the

top, she turned back and watched Claude climb into his car. Sad. That's what she felt. Sad that for a moment she'd been tricked—almost tricked. But no big loss. She had known there was always a catch with him. Anyway, he hadn't taken it back—the offer to use the sub.

She watched him pull away, slamming the four-wheel drive into gear like an overgrown hot-rod kid.

Mary Beth shook her head, then looked at her watch. Thinking about kids, where were hers? She had told them just down the block.

There sure was no sign of them.

She looked across the street.

No sign of Terry, either, or that old motorcycle he'd been working on.

She sighed. She hoped she hadn't given Terry the wrong idea about her and Claude. But she didn't want Terry to get the wrong idea about her and him, either— her and Terry, that is. It had been a nice day out on the boat. But that was all. There was no her and him.

She frowned and looked across at the driveway again.

The motorcycle was gone. He was gone.

That was okay with her.

Then why did she feel so forlorn all of a sudden?

# Chapter
## 10

Down the street, Jordan was madly pedaling his bike, towing the girls along on their skates, heading for the construction site, Zeus trotting happily alongside them.

The construction site was one of their favorite places to blade, but it was a little tricky. There were No Trespassing signs everywhere, and sometimes guards would come along out of nowhere. But it also had the best spot for blading, a huge concrete pipe that Judith and Nora and their friends spun through as if they were in an amusement park or something.

Jordan stopped at the gate, and the girls squeezed through, then rolled away from him, waving, joining some others who were already there.

"Later!" Judith called.

Jordan waved back.

"Come on, Zeus," Jordan said. "Follow me. One of these days, you and I are going to do that. I'll take a picture of you, Zeus, okay?"

Zeus barked his approval, then followed Jordan as he rode around the fence till he could see the far end of the big concrete tube. He crouched down, and watched as the girls zoomed on through.

They bladed into the tube like some wild things, flipping and circling.

Once, when Judith looked up and saw Jordan watching, she gave him a fast thumbs-up, then did a huge spin for him.

Jordan took a deep breath. "Look at that, Zeus," he said.

Zeus barked approvingly.

"Hey!" someone yelled.

Jordan spun around.

A huge security guard was tearing out of his guard house, heading straight toward the kids in the tube.

"Get!" he yelled. "What are you kids doing? Get out of there. Now!"

"Uh-oh," Jordan muttered. He cupped his hands to his mouth. "Come on, you guys!" he yelled. "Nora! Judith! This way."

He bent to pick up his bike, but when he looked again, the girls weren't coming his way. Instead, they had skated to the end of the pipe and out and were heading across the field to the open gate on the far side.

Dummies! You couldn't skate in a field.

The guard was right on their tail, closing in on them.

Jordan watched, horrified. Zeus watched, too, whining, whimpering with fear.

Then Jordan saw something else. A police car. A police car had pulled up at the far gate.

Judith and Nora couldn't have seen it yet. Could they? They should turn. But no, it wouldn't matter if they did, because the guard was behind them now and the police in front.

And then— Oh, no!

"Zeus!" Jordan yelled.

Zeus had left his side and was chasing the police, barking and yapping.

"Come back here!" Jordan yelled. "You can't stop them. There's too many of them."

But he didn't go after Zeus. He knew Zeus was faster than any guard or police officer. Zeus would get back to him. Anyway, Jordan was pretty sure police didn't arrest dogs.

He wasn't too sure about kids, though.

He frowned as he followed the progress of his friends.

Across the field, Judith and her friends had reached the open gate, but she was suddenly tumbling, careening out of control. Then, even from that far away, he could hear the sound—somebody crashing into the hood of the police car.

He squinched up his eyes.

Busted.

He took a deep breath. Looked for Zeus.

As if Jordan's thought had summoned him up, Zeus was suddenly right there, right by his feet.

"Come on, dog!" Jordan said. "Let's go."

He hopped on his bike. How to help his friends? He couldn't leave them in this mess. They were in trouble. *Deep* trouble.

If only . . .

Then he saw him—Terry. His dad. Relief flooded him. His dad could help. Terry could do anything. Well, almost anything.

He was riding by on his motorcycle, but at the sight of the police cars, he slowed, then stopped.

"Hey!" Jordan yelled, waving to him. "Hey!"

Terry looked around and saw him. "What is it?" he said. His face was suddenly a mask of fear. "Are you all right? What happened?"

Jordan nodded. "Fine," he said. "Sort of. But my friends, Judith, Nora?" He made a motion with his thumb. "They're getting busted."

Terry looked where Jordan pointed. "Oh, boy," he said.

"Terry?" Jordan said.

"Yes?"

"I think this is their first offense," Jordan said. "We can probably get them off with a stern warning."

Terry smiled at his son.

Jordan smiled back.

"Come on," Terry said. He made room, and Jordan dropped his bike and hopped on behind his dad.

Together, with Zeus following along, they went to face the police officers.

When they got there, Jordan stood aside, watching. His dad was definitely doing the dad thing—talking seriously to the officers, frowning hard at Judith and Nora.

Jordan couldn't hear what they were saying, but he could tell it was working by the way the officers were nodding and listening. Every so often, one of them would look at Nora or Judith.

Jordan looked, too.

Boy, did Judith and Nora look ticked off. They should look sad or forlorn or sorry or something. Even though

Jordan had never been busted, still he knew that. That's what the police wanted.

Still, Terry's talking seemed to work. Because in just a minute, they were out of there—all of them, girls and all.

Jordan hopped on his bike, and the two girls got on behind Terry as they headed home.

Zeus trotted along beside, barking every little while.

When they finally stopped, just around the corner from their houses, and piled off, Judith turned to Terry. "Hey," she said. "Uh, thanks for talking Deputy Dawg out of serious jail time."

"You're welcome," Terry answered with a smile.

"That's all?" Nora said. She backed up a bit, tilted her head to one side. "That can't be all. What's the catch?"

"No catch," Terry said.

Judith made a face. "Yeah," she said. "Except for a lecture, right?"

"Nah," Jordan said. "He's not very good at those."

"Except I'm going to try," Terry said suddenly. He looked hard at the girls then. "Look," he said, "there are so many ways to have fun without getting into trouble."

"Right," Nora said. "Except Mom's not interested in us having fun."

"Yeah," Judith said. "It's the reason she lives, to keep us from having fun. Well, that and her work."

"Come on, give her a break," Terry said. "What I'm trying to say is, there are ways to have fun without putting yourselves in a spot like this."

"Oh, right!" Judith said. "Like we knew the cops were going to be there."

Nora looked at her sister. "He really acts like a dad, you know?" she said.

65

Both girls turned to Jordan. He just shrugged.

"Well, not like our dad," Judith said.

Terry raised his eyebrows.

"He's remarried," Judith said.

"Yeah," Nora said. "To Gwen. She's from Texas."

Judith made a face at her sister. "No, she's not!" she said. "She's from New Jersey."

Nora shrugged. "She looks like she's from Texas," she said.

Judith put out her hands, about a foot from her head on either side. "Big hair," she said.

"She used to be a cheerleader," Nora said. "Or something."

Terry nodded.

"She's always on a diet, too," Judith said.

"Always steaming vegetables," Nora added.

Judith made a little breath, almost like a sigh. "We don't see them much," she said.

Terry nodded slowly. "I guess that's a bummer," he said.

"Nope!" Judith said.

"We don't like steamed vegetables," Nora added.

"Oh," Terry said. "And that's it, huh? No regrets?"

He looked from one girl to the other. They both shrugged casually, but in their faces there was something else. Sadness? Something.

"Come on," Terry said quietly. "Let's go home."

Slowly, he pushed the bike the rest of the way.

As they came around the corner, Judith nudged Nora and pointed. There was Mary Beth about to get in her car, keys in hand, looking frantically up and down the street. When she saw the girls, she shouted, "Do you girls know what time it is!"

Judith turned to Jordan. "I think it's time for the Marlins game on your TV satellite dish," she said.

Jordan nodded. "Yeah," he said. "Let's go."

Then all three of them raced up the steps to Jordan's house.

Mary Beth left her car and headed over to Terry. "Tell me they weren't robbing a bank," she said.

"No." Terry shook his head, looked up at the kids. "No. They were not robbing a bank."

"He'll probably bust us," Judith called from the porch.

"Not Terry," Jordan answered.

Terry turned to Mary Beth. "Listen," he said. "I know it's not easy, putting in the hours you do and raising them."

Mary Beth sighed. "Not easy?" she said. "Nothing's easy with them. Know what? They won't do anything with me anymore. They even refuse to set foot on my boat anymore."

"They do?" Terry said. "How come?"

"They say I turn everything into a science lesson," she answered.

"Do you?" Terry asked.

She shrugged, tried to smile. "Maybe," she said. "Nora told me the other day that I treat her and Judith like lab rats. Research and results, she said, that's all I care about." She sighed. "Maybe it's my training, I don't know. But I guess I'm not as fun as I could be."

Terry nodded. "Maybe I'm not either." He took her hand, pulled her down onto the porch step beside him. "How about this?" he said. "How about I take the girls out fishing tomorrow. Give you a little bit of a break?"

Mary Beth looked at him, eyebrows up.

67

"It'd be a break for me, too," Terry said. "Really. See, this music, this composition, it's driving me crazy."

Mary Beth smiled. "You'd do that for them?" she asked.

Terry nodded. "Sure," he said. "They seem to need a—"

He stopped. A dad, is what he was about to say. But instead he said, "A friend."

"Somebody other than a borderline juvenile delinquent, you mean," Mary Beth said with a sigh.

They sat side by side quietly for a while.

"Know what?" Mary Beth said after a while. "I don't want to lose them. I just don't know how to be a mother to teenagers, I guess."

Terry laughed, took her hand, and squeezed it. "That's all right. Nobody knows how to do that. It's just trial and error. But they're good kids. They think the world of you. I can tell."

"I don't know," she said.

He was still holding her hand, and she didn't pull away.

After a minute, Terry turned to the house, looked up at the windows. He frowned. Were those faces he saw there in the window—kids' faces—just before the curtain dropped suddenly?

"Call me paranoid," he said. "But somehow I get the feeling we're being watched."

Mary Beth turned too, frowned, turned back. "With those two girls, I feel like that all the time."

And they weren't wrong about being watched. Through binoculars, too. All three kids. Cheering them on.

68

# Chapter
# 11

Judith had first turn. She held the binoculars to her eyes and peered through them. "They're still talking!" she said, incredulous.

Nora grabbed the binoculars from her. "Give me those," she said. "I can lip read."

She held the binoculars to her face. She saw Terry move closer to Mary Beth. Apparently unconsciously, Mary Beth moved toward him. The space between them was very, very small. And they were holding hands.

"Whoa!" Nora yelled. "Who cares about reading lips? I'm reading body language, and they're talking a mile a minute."

"What are they saying?" Jordan said.

Nora turned and looked at him. She grinned.

Judith did, too.

Then both of them turned back to the window.

"You're too young," Nora said.

And that's how come, on Saturday night, Mary Beth

was standing in her room, modeling a long evening dress, turning this way and that, studying herself in the mirror.

She turned to Nora and Judith, who were lounging on her bed, watching her. The room looked as if a tornado had hit and flung out every item of clothing in her closet—jeans, skirts, shirts.

"What do you think?" she said, looking at the girls.

Nora shook her head.

"Why not?" Mary Beth said.

"Jeans," Nora said.

"Right," Judith said.

"But this is a real date," Mary Beth said. "I'm wearing a real dress."

"Mo-om!" Judith said. "On a motorcycle?"

She grabbed a pair of jeans from the bed, threw them to her mother. "Put these on," she said. "You wait and see. Jeans. Terry'll be wearing jeans."

"And a leather jacket," Nora said.

"Definitely," Judith said.

"How can you be so sure?" Mary Beth said.

"Trust us, Mom," Nora said.

Mary Beth shook her head, but she let the girls help her off with the dress. When she had pulled on her jeans, she definitely felt better—more like herself.

She crossed the room, peeked out the front window. Across the street, Terry was standing by his bike with his neighbor Mrs. Rice, who owned the rotten cat. Jordan was there, too, Zeus in his arms. Why'd they all have to be out there like that? Like an entire welcoming committee.

Terry was wearing jeans and a leather jacket.

Mary Beth turned and squinched up her eyes at her daughters. "Think you're so smart," she muttered. But then she gave them a big smile and a kiss good-bye and she started across the street. Her heart was pounding wildly in her throat.

A date. A real date.

It had been a long time. She hadn't known she'd be this nervous.

Terry was nervous, too, she could tell. He started to talk when she was still halfway across the street. "Hey!" he called. "You look really—"

He stopped. Looked at Jordan. At Mrs. Rice. At Zeus. Back at Mary Beth.

"Nice," he said. "You look really nice."

"Thanks," Mary Beth said.

"Jordan," Terry said suddenly. "Now, I want you to listen to everything that Mrs. Rice says. Hear?"

Jordan's eyebrows went up. "Uh, sure," he said. "Father. Sir."

Terry nodded, turned to Mrs. Rice. "We won't be late," he said.

"Fine, fine," Mrs. Rice said.

"And Judith and Nora can come over?" Jordan said.

"They're grounded," Mary Beth said. She looked at Terry, then added, "Well, all right. If it's all right with Mrs. Rice?"

"Fine, fine," Mrs. Rice said again.

Terry handed Mary Beth a helmet, then settled himself on the bike.

Carefully, Mary Beth climbed on behind him, pulling on the helmet. "I'm so glad I combed my hair," she muttered.

Suddenly, the bike roared to life. Mary Beth turned to

71

wave good-bye. As she did, she heard something and she hoped desperately Terry hadn't heard it, too.

Mrs. Rice. Mrs. Rice, who could obviously say more than fine, fine, was saying, loud and clear, "Nothing so wonderful as young love."

In just a few minutes Terry pulled into the parking lot of a restaurant and disco place—Banana Bay Restaurant and Club, it said on the sign overhead.

They went inside, each of them being careful not to touch, to get too close.

Once inside, Mary Beth noticed how Terry kept looking around, as if he was looking for someone. Or something.

Nervous, that's all, she decided. He was as nervous as she. How come? Guys were supposed to be cool, weren't they?

However, when they were seated and served, and when they had something to do with their hands, they both seemed to relax a bit. Mary Beth spoke first.

"So," she said. "Tell me about Zeus. How did you get him?"

"Oh," Terry said, smiling. "Famous story. See, it was a dark and stormy night. Jordan and I were driving down a deserted road by a cornfield. There was an incredible flashing light in the sky and a meteorite came thundering down ahead of us. We ran into the field and there—"

"Was Zeus!" Mary Beth interrupted, laughing.

"Right," said Terry. "Wrapped in a Marlins blanket and—"

"No!" Mary Beth said. "A Dolphins blanket!"

"Right!" Terry said again. He shook his head. "Now,

if only I could do as well with inventing my music, my opera."

"What's your opera about?" Mary Beth asked.

Terry made a face. "About six weeks late," he answered.

Mary Beth raised her eyebrows.

"What?" Terry said.

"A little evasive, aren't we?" she said.

Terry looked down into his drink, picked up the little umbrella that had come with it, turned it round and round. "I don't mean to be," he said. "It's just that the music is evasive, too. I suppose the opera's about love." He gave her a lopsided smile. "Along with the requisite over-the-top pyrotechnics."

She smiled back. "And with the requisite happy ending?" she asked.

"I don't know yet," Terry said. He frowned at her. "I don't know yet."

For a long minute, they held each other's eyes, until Mary Beth turned away.

She looked out at the dance floor. People were out there dancing—well, sort of dancing. They looked like acrobats, twisting, ducking.

"Limbo," Terry said, as though he was reading her mind.

"Oh," she said.

"Want to try it?" he said.

"Oh, no!" she said. "I mean, well, my back doesn't have a lot of flexibility right now."

Terry picked up the tiny umbrella, fiddled with it again. "So," he said, not looking at her. "This Claude guy? Do you . . . like . . . see him?"

Mary Beth laughed. "Every day," she said.

"Oh," he said. "Really."

"Really," she said. "He's one of the head honchos at the ocean complex. I used to be his assistant, until we had a parting of the ways."

Terry looked up. "Would it be tactless to ask over what?" he said.

Mary Beth smiled, and then, for some reason, she couldn't help teasing him. "Over a third party," she said gravely.

"Oh," he said. "Sorry. Never mind. You don't have to—"

Mary Beth grinned at him, put a hand on his arm. "No, it's all right. I was teasing. It was over a dolphin. I thought the dolphins were more important than his career."

Terry smiled at her, a really incredible smile. When he leaned in close to her, she could smell his aftershave, his—

She shouldn't be thinking like this. She shook her head and turned away. Before she could think of anything more to say, this conga line went snaking past, and someone reached down and grabbed her hand.

Suddenly, she and Terry were both on their feet, holding hands and laughing. Laughing. Until the music changed. A slow dance, one of those close-up and intimate ones.

Terry turned to Mary Beth. She moved into his arms, yet she could feel a part of herself holding back, away from him.

Roxanne. Strange. But Roxanne was there in her head. Roxanne who couldn't trust, either, who held back.

Mary Beth sighed, turned her head so it was resting on Terry's shoulder. Forced herself to move closer.

"So," Terry said. "You said that dolphins are telepathetic."

"Yup."

"How about people?" he said.

Mary Beth looked up at him. "Some people," she said.

He pulled her closer and smiled.

Then, somehow, she let herself go. She let herself relax in his arms, let herself feel something for the first time in a very long time.

Then the dance was over, the night was over, and before they knew it, they were home.

"That was nice," Mary Beth said as they climbed off the bike and stood facing each other.

"I really enjoyed it," Terry said.

Mary Beth made a wry face. "You sound surprised," she said.

"I am," Terry said. He frowned. "Hey, wait a minute!" Heat flooded his face. "I didn't mean it like that."

Mary Beth nodded. "Good," she said.

And then—why not?—she leaned across the bike and kissed him. Hard.

His arms went around her.

And he kissed her back. Hard.

If either had been thinking, they would have realized that, just like last time, they were being spied upon. All three kids were watching from the window of Jordan's house.

"She is really into it!" Nora was saying.

"My dad!" Jordan said. "Mister Velocity. I don't believe it."

"And my mom usually scores such dorks!" Judith said.

"This looks pretty serious," Nora added.

Judith turned, smiled at Jordan. "I see a new brother in our future," she said. She frowned at him. "He won't dump her, will he?"

Jordan shrugged. "Who knows what will happen in the Terry Zone?" he said. "See, it's hard for him. Your mom is the first since—"

He stopped.

Judith turned, looked at him. Nora did, too.

Tears? Were those tears in his eyes?

Both girls reached out for him, hugged him, wrapped their arms around him in a three-way hug.

"It's okay, Jordan," Judith said softly.

"It is," Nora added.

Jordan wriggled out of their arms, rubbed a hand across his eyes.

Weird. He'd never been hugged by girls before. Even weirder, it felt kind of good.

All three of them turned back to the window.

"Look at that, will you?" Judith said.

"They're really hugging!" Nora said. "No holding back there."

"Have you children no decency?" Mrs. Rice said suddenly. She had appeared from behind them, and she reached across, pulling the curtains shut. "Really."

Judith and Nora and Jordan looked at one another. Zeus whimpered pitifully.

Mean. It was really mean. They were shut out of all the fun.

# Chapter
## 12

Zeus was at the marine center and on board the *Daily Planet* early next morning, panting in his excitement to go out and see Roxanne again.

But Zeus wasn't the only person aboard the *Daily Planet.*

Claude Carver had been there for several hours ahead of him, silently, sneakily, going through Mary Beth's notebooks and tapes. Every so often, he would stop, whip out a tiny camera, and take a photo of a particular page. Page after page, notebook after notebook, he photographed. He had done just about all the books, when he heard footsteps and the scampering of paws.

He peered through the window—saw feet—Becky's feet. Or was that Mary Beth?

Claude crouched.

Now what?

Where to go?

Then, to his enormous relief, the footsteps went the other way, below deck, away from the tiny office where he crouched.

He was out of here. Now. He bent, grabbed his briefcase, then scurried out onto the bridge of the boat.

And right into Zeus.

Zeus growled, low, menacingly.

"Hush, doggie," Claude whispered. He put a finger to his lips. "Please, doggie."

But Zeus began barking ferociously, a loud, ominous sound, then lowered himself close to the ground, snarling.

"Zeus?" Becky called. "Zeus? What is it?"

Suddenly, Zeus rushed Claude, sinking his teeth into Claude's pant leg.

Claude started to let out a yelp but stifled it. Footsteps were coming his way. Becky. Coming up the steps.

"Zeus?" she called again.

Claude backed up around the corner of the boat's cabin, away from the footsteps, dragging Zeus, who was still clinging to his pant leg.

He could hear Becky on deck, hear and even feel her footsteps coming closer. "Zeus?" she called.

Claude bent, reached for Zeus, his face a mask of anger and pain. He tried desperately to loosen Zeus's grip. "Let go! Stop!" he commanded under his breath "Leave off!" He grabbed Zeus's neck and shook him hard.

Suddenly, Claude was drenched, a huge wave of water washing over him.

He let go of Zeus, spun around, and saw a dolphin, right up close.

Roxanne. She slapped her tail on the water. Slapped hard. Again. And again. And again. Drenching him.

Claude put an arm across his face, shielding himself. He shook his head, shaking the water from his face and eyes.

"Zeus?" Becky called. She was right there, right around the corner of the cabin.

Claude bent once more, grabbed Zeus hard, and shoved him backward, finally dislodging him. Then snatching up his metal briefcase, he leaped for his boat, which was docked just on the other side.

Only he missed. He grabbed for a pylon with one hand. And fell fast, disappearing under the murky water.

Just as Becky came around the corner.

She put her hands on her hips, looking first at Zeus, then at Roxanne. "What is it with you two?" she said. "What's going on here?"

Zeus barked. Roxanne *blatted.*

Becky made a face. "Same to you," she said. "Now, behave. Both of you." Then she turned and went back belowdecks to her work.

Claude slowly came up to the surface. He tossed his briefcase onto the deck of his boat, climbed up after it— and saw Phil and Linda there, both of them watching him.

"Looks like you need a towel," Phil said calmly.

"No big deal," Claude said. He climbed over the railing and onto the deck, nonchalant, as if this was something he did every day. "A little slip, that's all," he said, wiggling his fingers at them. He twisted some water from his shirt. "And yes," he added. "I do need a towel. Thanks."

79

Phil turned away, headed belowdecks to the storage cabinet, Linda following.

"He looks like the Creature from the Black Lagoon," Phil muttered to her.

Linda grinned. "Saw all his movies," she said.

Phil laughed, got a towel from the cabinet, and shook it out. But when he turned back to Linda, he wasn't smiling. "Okay," he said quietly. "But what was that all about? What's the Creature from the Black Lagoon doing—with his briefcase—on Mary Beth Dunhill's boat?"

"Research?" Linda said.

"Yeah," Phil said. "You can believe that. And you can bet it's not his own."

Linda nodded.

"I'm waiting for that towel!" Claude yelled from above them.

They waited just one moment longer. Then they took the towel up on deck, where Claude stood, dripping.

"Follow me," Claude said after he had wiped most of the water from his face and arms. "And Linda? I hope you did what I said. You have the dogs?"

She nodded. "I have them."

"Good. Get them ready," he said.

Once they were back inside the research center, Claude went to his office, closed himself in, taking a quick minute to look at the notes he had stolen from Mary Beth. Through a window, he watched as Linda picked up a small yellow dog and cuddled it to her.

He stared again at the notes, shaking his head. "So she won't share, will she?" he muttered. "Well, neither will I. I'll surpass her feeble attempts at interspecies communication. They'll have no choice but to give me the grant."

He took a deep breath, then stuffed the notes into his desk and locked it. Then he smoothed out his shirt and pants as best he could, and went out to join Linda and Phil, who were waiting by the dolphin pens.

Claude noddly curtly and pointed at the dog that Linda held. "Let's start with her," he said. "She's sickeningly cuddly enough. Go on."

Slowly, carrying the little dog, Linda climbed up onto a platform above the main dolphin tank.

Below her, Claude signaled for Phil. "Okay. Release her!" he shouted.

Phil nodded, then opened the gate.

A dolphin splashed into the water. She raised an enormous swell in the tank, flapping her huge tail.

The little dog trembled, then began to bark nervously.

Linda set the dog down on the platform. "It's all right," she said to her. "Nothing bad's going to happen."

Except it did. The dolphin leaped high in the air. High. Then dove under water, sending cascades of water everywhere.

That's when the little dog really went wild. She fled from the platform, scrambled away from Linda, and in a minute was on her way out through an open door, all the time barking wildly.

Linda ran after her, and Phil also came running.

"Quick!" Linda yelled. "This way! Get her."

They both raced through the open door and out to the dock.

Nothing. No dog. Gone. Then Linda pointed. "There," she said softly.

The little dog was cowering in a corner, shivering. Very slowly, Linda approached her. She bent, picked her up, held her close. "It's okay," she murmured soothingly. "It's all right."

"Not really," Phil said. "What do you think Claude'll do next?"

"Claude?" she said. "Knowing him, he'll want another dog. Let's go."

They went back into the center, where Linda returned the little dog to her cage, then called down to Claude. "What now?"

"The hound!" he said.

Linda nodded. She went back to the row of cages and opened one where a short, stubby, sad-faced hound dog cowered. "Don't worry," she said, reaching in and pulling him gently toward her. "I'm right here."

She carried the dog out to the platform, high above the dolphin pens, then set him down.

The hound crouched, shivered, looked down. Then he looked up at Linda, his eyes sad, pleading almost, it seemed. He hunkered down on the platform, his eyes swiveling this way, that, anxious. Linda could see his chest heaving, see the thump of his heartbeat in his throat.

Linda put a hand on the dog's head. "It's all right," she said. "I'm here. You're safe."

But the hound didn't seem to think so. The minute Phil released the dolphin into her pen, the dog threw back his head and set up a wild howling. The sound echoed through the hall, a long, mournful wail. A mournful wail that was taken up by every other dog in the area.

82

"Enough!" Claude yelled. "Get rid of that one." He put his hands over his ears. "Get the monkey!" he shouted to Phil. "Bring her down on this level. Maybe it's the height that's bothering them."

Linda picked up the hound, held him close to her, cuddling him, soothing him. "It's okay," she murmured. "It is. Come on. Let's watch."

She backed off the platform and stood on the balcony above the pen, the dog still in her arms. She watched as Phil sent another dolphin through the gates of the pen. This one, just like the last, immediately dove and disappeared.

"She'll resurface," Claude yelled. "Let out the monkey. On this level. Let her get eye to eye with the dolphin when she comes up."

Phil nodded, opened a gate for the monkey. The monkey ambled out, looked around, her quick little eyes taking in everything.

She wandered over to the edge of the pool, looked in. Nothing. The dolphin was still under water.

The monkey then turned around and scooted backward, eyeing Claude, then ran right up to him. Her brown eyes blinked rapidly as she looked Claude over.

For a moment, they stared at each other. And then, the monkey ran to the pool again, again looked down.

The dolphin was still in hiding.

Back and forth the monkey ran, from Claude to the pool, from the pool to Claude. Then, as if the monkey knew something was down there hiding, she ran to the pool again, leaned far out over the water, and peered down.

Just as the dolphin surfaced.

Her mammoth head came above the water. There it was, huge face, enormous eyes—right in the monkey's face.

For one moment, nothing happened. Both creatures were still.

And then the monkey began backpedaling. She made frantic sounds, tiny squeaky, helpless sounds.

She looked around. Eyed Claude. Ran.

She leaped straight into his arms and buried her head in his chest.

# Chapter
# 13

Terry sat on the back porch, noodling around with his guitar, Mary Beth by his side. She was relaxed, shoes off, feet up on a table, looking out at the bay.

It was late evening, after a full day's work for both of them. As far as Terry was concerned, it was work with little accomplished. The melody was still eluding him. For Mary Beth, though, it had been a good day. Jordan and Zeus had been out on her boat, and there was no doubt that dog and dolphin were communicating. Mary Beth had a whole tape full of sounds, play, interaction.

Besides, Mary Beth couldn't help noticing that Jordan was a neat kid. Really insightful.

She sneaked a look at Terry. Were they alike, Jordan and Terry? Or were they as different as dads and sons sometimes were?

No way to know for sure, was there? Not yet, anyway.

The only thing she could tell for sure now, was that

Terry was frowning, frowning hard, as he plucked at the guitar.

"A bad time?" she said quietly.

He nodded. "Lately, it's all a bad time. I always thought writer's block was a myth, an excuse to goof off. Except I don't want to goof off. And I still can't find this melody."

Mary Beth smiled. "Maybe it will be all the sweeter when you do."

Terry smiled back, shrugged. "Maybe," he said, and he plinked some more at his guitar.

Mary Beth turned back to the bay, thinking she saw something moving out there. She put up a hand to shade her eyes.

Yes. There was something out there. Dolphins. A whole pod of dolphins. Roxanne's pod? Way out on the horizon, they were moving along the surface of the water, leaping, diving, cavorting. As she watched, they moved closer to shore, swimming together in unison. She had to smile. They looked as if they were on a family outing, just hanging out with each another, chattering, playing.

Mary Beth turned to Terry and pointed. "I think the dolphins hear your music."

Terry looked where she was pointing. "All right," he said. "I'll sing to them." He smiled, made some sounds with his guitar—a twang and a pop, another twang and pop.

The dolphins came closer.

"Do it again," Mary Beth said.

Terry did—twanged and popped.

Closer. The dolphins swam even closer.

Mary Beth softly clapped her hands. "I know they hear you!" she said gleefully.

Terry looked down at his guitar and made more popping, blatting sounds.

And then, suddenly, it wasn't just popping and blatting sounds he was making. It was more like—yes, it was—more like a melody. A melody that began to form itself, not a blat or a squawk, but one note that merged with another, then another, then more, stringing themselves together, more and more. A melody was forming. It welled up, escaping the guitar, as though creating itself.

Terry took a deep breath and closed his eyes, almost afraid to breathe. He plucked carefully at the strings, his fingers looking for something—something that was there, something that was forming all by itself.

He breathed deep, sent a look to Mary Beth.

It was happening. The melody was happening!

"I think it's working," he whispered.

He played some more, felt it swelling, rushing, as if creating itself from the heart of the guitar.

"It's working!" he said then. "I know it!"

Out there on the horizon, the dolphins seemed to know it, too. They joined in with a huge chorus of sounds, bleeping, blatting, squawking. Singing almost.

Then they leaped in the air, like an incredible ballet, dove under and resurfaced, just as Terry found a chord, a series of chords, and filled the air with music, with joy.

He was smiling, smiling. "I've found my melody," he whispered.

"You've found yourself a band, I think," Mary Beth said, nodding toward the dolphins in the bay.

Terry laid the guitar down gently, laughing. He waved

out toward the sea. "Good job, mates!" he called to the dolphins. "Rehearsal tomorrow. Same time. Same place!"

He turned, laughing, to Mary Beth, then stopped when he saw the somber look on her face.

"What's wrong?" he said. "What is it?"

"Roxanne," Mary Beth answered. "That was her pod, her family. She's too frightened to join them."

Terry reached over and took her hand, held it gently. "Why?" he said. "What happened to make her afraid?"

"She had a traumatic experience in her past," Mary Beth said, her face pulled into a frown, remembering Claude and his experiments with dolphins.

Terry nodded, then turned away to look out to sea. "I know how she feels," he said softly.

"I do, too," Mary Beth answered. "But somehow I have to make her realize that things can be okay again."

"Can they?" Terry said, still looking out to sea. "And how do you make her realize that?"

She shrugged, sighed. "Not sure," she said. "Trust is a funny thing. But her relationship with Zeus is an important first step in that, in trusting."

Terry smiled. "Then thank goodness for Zeus," he said.

"Yes," Mary Beth said. "But something happened today. Roxanne almost got caught in a net. Just what she didn't need—more trauma."

Terry frowned. "A net? What net?"

"Drift nets," Mary Beth said. "Poachers. They kill hundreds of dolphins a year."

She looked up at him. "Jordan was with me. We led Roxanne away from it. I let him go down with me in the sub. Know what he said to me?"

88

Terry laughed. "Knowing Jordan, it could have been anything," he said.

"He thanked me," she said.

"For taking him down?"

Mary Beth shook her head and looked down at their intertwined hands. "No," she said, very softly. "Thanked me for helping you. He thinks this is helping your music."

Terry held her hand more tightly.

"I don't want to say good-bye to you, Terry," Mary Beth said.

He squeezed her hand harder. "Me neither," he said. "When do you have to move? When's the rental up?"

"Friday," Terry said. "I even asked about extending the lease, but we can't. There's a new family coming in Saturday morning. Then it's back to Boca Raton for a week, where I'll mix my tracks for the music."

"Then?" Mary Beth said.

"Back to Boston." Terry sighed. "My real job. School for Jordan." He stared down at their hands some more, twined his fingers tight inside of hers. "What about you?"

"I stay here for the rest of the summer," she answered. "That is, if I get the grant. Then I can continue through the winter and complete my research."

"And if you don't get the grant?" Terry said.

Mary Beth shrugged. "Then it's home to Minnesota, being a tour guide at the aquarium." She loosened her hand from Terry's, stood up, and looked across the street at her house. "And hoping the girls do all right with all the moving around," she added.

She looked back at Terry. "So, what are we going to do about this?" she said suddenly. "About you? Me?"

She turned away quickly, feeling the heat come up her cheeks, her neck. She hadn't meant to say it out loud, hated herself for her impulsiveness.

For a long time, there was just silence.

Then, behind her, she heard Terry's answer, soft as could be, so soft she could barely hear him.

"I don't know," he said. "I just don't know."

# Chapter
## 14

Jordan and Judith and Nora didn't know, either. But that didn't stop them from trying to figure it out.

They huddled together at Jordan's house that night, planning, cooking up schemes. Jordan was setting up to take pictures—he did a great shot of Zeus, all dressed up like GI Joe.

Jordan pretended to be stern, putting one hand under Zeus's chin. "Come on, soldier!" he said. "Pull yourself together!"

But he knew he was really talking to himself. Even though they'd hung out for hours, at bedtime they still hadn't come up with one single plan that would work.

Next morning, they tried again, meeting on the beach. Still talking. Still worrying. They even played a few hands of poker, which Nora and Judith had taught Jordan. He was awfully good at it. The only betting they did was on who did whose chores, and so far, the girls were Jordan's slaves for the summer. But even that wasn't any fun that morning.

"You can't go!" Nora said.

"Yeah," Jordan said. "I know." He heaped sand on Zeus, burying him. "I don't want to. Terry hasn't been this good, hasn't been able to create music like this since—"

He stopped, poked some more sand down around Zeus's paws.

He always had to stop, swallow hard, whenever he got to this part, even inside his own head.

"So rent another place," Nora said.

"Can't," Jordan said. "We tried. And Terry tried to extend the rental here, but no go."

"I know!" Judith said suddenly. "It's simple! Why didn't I think of it before?"

Jordan and Nora turned to her. Even Zeus looked at her.

"Jordan and Terry can stay with us!" Judith said, looking at her sister.

"Us?" Nora said.

"Why not? There's two extra bedrooms. Jordan could have one, and Terry could have the other."

Jordan shook his head. "No way. Terry would never go along with that."

"Bet he would," Judith said. She smiled at her sister. "If we did it right, he would."

"Ah, ha!" Nora said, smiling back at her sister. "We tell Terry it was her idea. Right?"

"Right!" Judith said.

"It was?" Jordan said. "You mean, she suggested it? She thought of it all by herself?"

Judith shook her head. "Course not," she said. "She doesn't know a thing about it."

"Yet," Nora said. "But she'll go along if we tell her it was Terry's idea."

"Wait a minute," Jordan said. "You mean, she's supposed to think he thought of it, and he's supposed to think—"

"Exactly," Judith said. She looked at her watch and stood up. "Come on, Nora," she said, tugging her sister to her feet. "Let's go. Almost lunch time. Let's go see Mom at work, tell her how much Terry wants to stay with us."

She turned to Jordan then, pointing a finger at him. "And you go to work on Terry. Okay? Be sure he understands that it was her idea."

Jordan stood up, too, dusted himself off, then freed Zeus from the sand.

"Okay," he said. "But if either of them finds out, we're dead. You know that."

"How are they going to find out?" Judith said. "See you."

She grabbed her sister's hand, and they headed toward their mom's work, hurrying to beat the clock. They knew Mary Beth—everything was on schedule. Her boat would dock at noon exactly, and at five minutes after, she'd be off and on her way to her favorite salad place for lunch.

It was just five till noon.

"Wait till Mom sees us showing up at her work," Nora said as they hurried to the complex. "Want to take bets on what she says?"

"I can think of two things," Judith said. "We burned down the school, or we're about to be hauled off to jail."

"I'm betting on the burning down the school part," Nora said.

In just a few minutes they were on the dock, looking out over the bay, eyes squinted up against the brilliant sun.

Judith looked at her watch. Noon. Exactly. Sure enough, the *Daily Planet* appeared, chugging in.

"Does she ever do anything off schedule?" Judith said.

"Couldn't if she tried," Nora answered.

As soon as the boat docked and was tied up, Mary Beth came racing down the gangplank and over to where they stood.

"What's the matter?" she said, reaching to hug them, then holding them away to look at them. "What happened?"

"Nothing," Judith answered.

"Why are you here, then?" Mary Beth asked.

Both girls shrugged.

Mary Beth folded her arms. "Did you burn down the school?" she said.

Nora grinned at her sister.

"We just wanted to have lunch with you, Mom," Judith said. "Come on. Aren't you happy to see us?"

Mary Beth gave them a look. But she walked along with them, all three of them heading for Mary Beth's favorite little outdoor restaurant.

When they had been served, Mary Beth looked from one to the other. "Okay," she said. "What's up?"

"Why does something have to be up?" Judith said. "We just wanted to see you."

Mary Beth shook her head. "Sorry," she said. "I know better. Besides, you both ordered salads."

"So?" Nora said. "You always eat salads."

"Yeah," Judith said. She bent over her lettuce, made a little face at it, but picked up her fork. "Why can't we eat salad, too?"

Mary Beth kept staring at them. "I get it," she said at last. "Satellite dish. You want a satellite dish. No way. We can't afford it."

"It's not the satellite dish," Judith said. She looked at her sister.

Nora looked back, nodded.

"Okay," Judith said, turning back to her mom. "See, it's Jordan and Terry. They need a place to live for a while."

"And we want them to stay at our house," Nora said.

Mary Beth frowned. "At our house? Terry?" She shook her head, "Unh-uh," she said.

"Why not?" Nora asked.

"No way," Mary Beth said. "Anyway, what makes you think they'd even want to stay at our house?"

"Jordan does," Nora said. "I know he does."

"And Terry does, too," Judith added.

"Says who?" Mary Beth asked, her eyes narrowed.

"Jordan," Judith said. "He just told us."

Nora nodded. "He tells us lots of stuff, really lots," she said, smiling.

"Wait a minute," Mary Beth said. "So Jordan's the one who said so."

"Yes!" Nora said. "Jordan. But it wasn't his idea. He said Terry suggested it. Jordan was just asking for him. You know Terry's shy."

Yes. She knew that.

And she knew something else—she didn't want to say good-bye to him. But did he really want to stay with her? Really?

And would that be all right with her? Could she do that?

She shook her head, took a bite of her salad, then another. It was all too confusing, too fast. Finally she said, "We'll talk about it later, okay?"

"Thanks, Mom!" Judith said. "I knew we could count on you."

"I didn't say yes," Mary Beth said.

"Yes, you did," Nora said.

Mary Beth sighed. She squinted at her daughters. After just a minute, she couldn't help starting to smile. Maybe she would say yes. She had told Terry that they had to do something about this, about him moving away. And now . . .

Now he had done something about it himself.

Yes. Maybe she would say yes.

# Chapter
## 15

By late the next afternoon, most of Terry's and Jordan's stuff had been packed. At least half of it stood around in boxes in doorways, on the porch, everywhere. Even the refrigerator had been cleaned out.

Terry had taken down the few pictures he'd brought with him, but he stood at the door to his room now, holding one in his hands, unable to put it in the box.

It was a picture of his wife. Jordan's mother.

He held the picture to himself, looked out the window across the street. How did he feel about sharing a house with Mary Beth and her daughters?

He shook his head.

Not sure. That's how he felt. He felt that he wasn't sure about how he felt. He smiled at himself, looked again at the picture.

He held it close again, closed his eyes, trying to feel the sense of her still. But there was no feeling from her. Gone. She was gone. How could she do that to him?

"Hey, Terry!" Jordan called from the kitchen. "What are you doing?"

"Nothing," Terry said. He put the picture on the bed, quickly slid it under a pile of shirts, and headed for the kitchen. "I'm starved," he said, throwing out his arms and stretching wide. "What's to eat?" He opened a cabinet, shut it, opened and shut another, looked around him.

Empty. All cleaned out.

He frowned at Jordan. "Where are my Twinkies?" he said.

Jordan rolled his eyes. "I made you a fruit salad. It's in the fridge."

Terry turned to the refrigerator, took out the salad, and turned back. He took a bite, then looked at Jordan. "Are you sure this was Mary Beth's idea?" he said. "This moving in over there?"

"Absolutely!" Jordan said. "Right, Zeus?"

Jordan bent and gave a grape to Zeus, who gulped it down, then yapped happily.

Jordan smiled. "See?" he said. "Even Zeus said so. And know what? He's happy."

Terry smiled. Zeus was happy. Jordan looked happy.

Terry frowned at his salad.

"Come on, Terry!" Jordan said. "Get a move on. There's another whole room to empty. But first, I want to move my photo stuff. You ready to help me?"

Terry took a few quick bites of his fruit salad, then set it down and grabbed one of the two huge boxes filled with Jordan's photo stuff.

"I'm ready," he said. And he followed Jordan across the street.

Up on the Dunhills' porch, Jordan set the box down

98

carefully, just as Judith appeared from around the corner of the house. She flipped a Frisbee to him.

Jordan grabbed it out of the air and flipped it back.

Nora appeared behind Judith, snagged the Frisbee, then turned and ran with it, racing to the back, out to the beach and along the sand.

Zeus followed, barking happily.

Jordan and Judith raced after them.

Terry couldn't help smiling. All the kids were happy. Even the dog. So?

"Terry?"

It was Mary Beth. She was standing in front of the porch, a watering can in her hand. "Terry?" she said again, laughing up at him. "Looks to me as if you're a bit overwhelmed."

He set down the box. "Yeah," he said. "Just daydreaming. Can't get anything done that way. And there's a ton to do."

"Walk on the beach?" Mary Beth suggested. "It helps me when I'm feeling overwhelmed."

Terry nodded, came down from the porch.

Together, they walked around the corner of the house and down to the beach. They watched the kids and Zeus chasing the Frisbee, but neither of them spoke.

After a few minutes, Terry could feel the quiet settling inside him, feel the peace of the water, the waves. It was nice here. Still, there were a few things he had to get settled, had to say out loud if they were going to do this living-in-the-same-house thing.

He shoved his hands into the pockets of his jeans. "Um, Mary Beth," he said. "There's a couple of things you should know about me."

She turned to him, laughing. "Like growing hair on your palms and baying at the full moon every month?"

Terry laughed, too. "Not exactly," he said. "But—"

"Hey," she said. "Too late to be reticent now. After all, this arrangement was your idea."

Terry stopped short and turned to face her. "Wait a minute," he said. "My idea? No way. Jordan—"

"Yes, way!" Mary Beth interrupted. "The girls said—"

"Jordan said—" Terry interrupted.

Then each stopped and looked at the other.

"Uh-oh," Mary Beth said.

"Uh-oh," Terry said back.

They turned, looked behind them.

Judith and Nora and Jordan were racing down the shoreline, Jordan waving the Frisbee, Zeus in pursuit.

For a long minute, neither Mary Beth nor Terry said anything.

Then Mary Beth pointed a finger to the kids. "We," she said, "have been set up."

"By world-class professionals," Terry added. "And they're going to hear about it."

They turned to each other.

"What do we do now?" Terry said.

Mary Beth took a deep breath. She looked at him for a long moment, then turned away and faced down the beach again, as if to continue their walk. "Well," she said slowly, "if you stay, I can continue my research with Zeus."

Terry nodded, started walking along beside her. "Yep. And I've got a second act to finish."

"So?" Mary Beth said. "Why don't we just try to make the best of it?"

Terry took her hand and stopped her. He turned her to face him. Softly, he said, "Why not?"

They both turned, facing back the way they had come, back to the kids. Back to moving the rest of the stuff.

And what a load of stuff they had. Amazing how much could be collected in just one short summer.

When they got back, Terry crossed the street to his house and began packing the last of his things. But when he got to that picture again, the one he had slid under the shirt pile, he found himself stuck again. Stuck staring at the picture. Just staring at it.

Maybe it was just the moving that was getting to him. Maybe it was because the picture made him remember all the times he and his wife had moved together.

He looked up and saw Jordan standing at the door to his room.

He slid the picture behind his back.

"Hey, Terry!" Jordan said. "Should I start carrying the rest of the stuff over there?"

Terry shook his head. "Let's get everything outside first," he said.

"How come?" Jordan said.

"Because I said so!" Terry snapped. "Okay?"

Jordan gave his father a long look. "Okay," he said quietly.

Jordan turned away, picked up a box, and took it to the porch. On the way, he passed Mary Beth, who was coming out on the porch, carrying some lemonade.

"Want some?" she said, smiling at him.

Jordan just shook his head and walked on past her.

Mary Beth gave him a look and shrugged. She went back into the house. "Terry?" she called.

He was still standing at the door to his room, his face

dark and sad. But he had put the picture on the bed behind him.

"Uh-oh," she said. "What happened?"

Terry shook his head. "Nothing."

"Okay," she said softly. "What didn't happen?"

But Terry had turned away.

Mary Beth put the lemonade on a table. "I think you ought to tell me," she said.

For what seemed like a full minute, Terry didn't speak. Finally he turned to face her. "I'm sorry," he said. "It's just—"

He paused.

She waited.

He sighed, then went on. "Well, are we doing this for the kids?" he asked. "Or for the Rockland Foundation? Or . . ." He paused, rubbed his hands hard over his face, as if he were wiping something away. "Or for us?" he added.

Mary Beth felt a tremor in her chest, a tightness. She looked down at the lemonade, watched the drops of condensation slide down the side of the pitcher.

She looked back up at him.

"I thought it was for all the above," she said quietly.

"Well," he said. "I don't know. I just don't know. But I do know I need the time to find out."

She nodded. "Okay," she said slowly. "Okay."

He took a step closer to her. "Listen, Mary Beth," he said.

But she stepped back, turned away.

For just a moment, she stood with her back to him, staring at the floor, at the ripple of light and shadows playing on the rug. She could feel the tremor of sadness in her chest swell, like a wave, an ocean.

102

"Take all the time you need, Terry," she said softly.

"But . . ." he said.

She went out then, heading for the porch.

He took a few steps after her, following her, but he stopped.

She was right. He was right. He did need time.

He waited till she was gone. Then slowly, he went outside, walked around back, headed out to the beach.

Far down along the shore, he could see the kids romping. Could hear Zeus rushing along the edge of the water, barking. Out in the water, he saw a dolphin— Roxanne?

Roxanne and Zeus seemed to be talking to one another, happily. Barking, yapping, blatting at one another.

They seemed to be getting along. He couldn't help thinking: so why can't we? A dog and a dolphin can get along, why can't the adults?

No answer to that one. He knew that for sure.

He wondered what would happen when he told Jordan.

Looking again down the beach, he realized the kids weren't frolicking at all. They were holding one another, all three of them. As he watched, he saw they were hugging. Probably, he figured, crying.

And he figured they had already figured it out.

# Chapter
## 16

Packing again. Going away. Not to Mary Beth and Nora and Judith. Going somewhere else. Far away.

Terry and Jordan piled in the pickup truck, but it took hours of driving, hours and hours of Zeus howling his anger and despair at the world. They were all three crammed into the cab of the pickup, their belongings piled high behind.

"Will you stop it!" Terry yelled at Zeus, finally. "I feel bad enough."

Zeus just howled again, louder even, as if he were arguing.

"I do," Terry repeated. "I feel awful."

Jordan kept one arm around Zeus, his head turned so that he was looking out the side window. "Then why don't you turn around?" he said, not looking at Terry.

Terry sighed. "I wish I could," he said.

Jordan rolled his eyes, but he didn't turn back to face his dad. "I don't see anyone else driving," he said.

"Jordan!" Terry said. "I . . ." He sighed. "Oh, forget it," he said. He reached over and flipped on the radio. Loud. To drown out Zeus's howls.

To cover Jordan's silence.

Maybe to cover up his own despair.

That's how they drove the whole night, radio blasting, Zeus growling. And Jordan and Terry as silent as death.

That's how it stayed, even after they got to their condo high above the beach. That was the only good thing about it—it was near the beach. A different beach. A lonely beach.

For days, the two of them stayed silent. Jordan could see that Terry was as lonely and lost feeling as he was, but being Terry, he wasn't going to admit it. And his music! It was awful. The melody had gone, had escaped him again completely.

You should ask me where it went, Jordan told him. But he didn't say it out loud, just inside his head.

Finally, one day, things came to a head—with Zeus, anyway. Terry was fiddling with his music, and it was so bad that Jordan had escaped.

He had taken a bunch of photographs and was holed up in the bathroom, using it as a dark room.

Outside the door, he could hear a ruckus, as if Zeus was into something. He heard barking. Wild barking. And Terry yelling.

And then, suddenly, the bathroom door was flung open and Terry stood there, outlined by the light. He had Zeus in his arms, practically strangling him. "In the cooler! Thirty days!" Terry yelled. And he practically threw Zeus into the bathroom.

"Dad!" Jordan yelled. "My pictures!"

"Sorry!" Terry said, but he didn't sound sorry. "You

can take more pictures. What am I saying? You *will* take more pictures."

He glared down at Zeus, who was backed up against Jordan's legs. "Just keep him out of my way. He's been biting my ankles. He pulled the plug on my amplifier. And now he's ruined my music! Tore up a whole sheet of it."

Good, Jordan thought. Your music stinks anyway.

He bent, picked up Zeus, and pushed past his dad. The pictures were ruined anyway. No sense hanging around to fix them.

"I'm taking Zeus out," he said. He gave his dad a look. "I think I need to reduce your coffee intake," he added.

Then he grabbed a fishing rod, and together he and Zeus headed for the beach.

For a long time, they walked along the beach, Jordan with the fishing rod, Zeus chasing sandpipers. Suddenly, Zeus went wild, barking and leaping.

Jordan looked up. "What?" he said. "What is it?"

Zeus yapped wildly, leaping up and down as if he were on little springs. He was staring straight out over the water.

Jordan turned and looked where he was looking.

Dolphins, there were dolphins out there, leaping from the water, skimming over the water, playing and cavorting.

Zeus barked wildly, leaping up and down, up and down.

Nothing. The dolphins paid him no attention at all.

That didn't stop Zeus, though. He just barked and barked, yapped and yipped. He made all the sounds he had made to Roxanne. He even howled, as if mimicking her whistle sound. But still nothing.

After a while, it became clear that the dolphins couldn't be coaxed into playing with him, weren't the least interested in his company, his sounds. Zeus stopped barking, stopped cavorting. Quietly, sadly, he watched.

Jordan bent and hugged him. "I know, buddy," he whispered to him. "I know."

They stood for a long time, watching while the dolphins played. When the dolphins finally dove and disappeared, they turned and headed for home.

Every little while, Zeus would look up at Jordan, as though asking a question.

But Jordan was too preoccupied to notice. Because he was thinking.

There had to be a way to fix this. There had to be.

Oddly, Zeus had the very same thought.

# Chapter
## 17

It was very early morning when Zeus made his move. He was on the balcony of the condo, the only place where he felt happy, since from there he could see out to the sea.

Behind him, Terry and Jordan were working, Terry at his music, his awful music. And Jordan at his photo collage.

Zeus paced back and forth, back and forth.

Out there, over the water, even from here, he could see the dolphins playing.

His dolphin?

No. He knew which one was Roxanne, and she was somewhere else. She was back where they had come from.

So there was only one thing to do. Go there. Go back to where she was. And since Jordan would never let him out, just to run free, there was only one way to do it. He leaped onto a chair. Looked over the rail.

He looked behind him again.

Terry was still plugged into his guitar, his ears covered with headphones. Jordan was still working on his photos.

Zeus turned back. Down below, a few floors below, he could see the swimming pool, see a few men already out there playing cards.

Well, he'd had some experience swimming recently.

He scrambled to the rail, his tail waving in a mad effort to keep his balance. He gathered himself together and leaped. Leaped straight down. Straight for the pool.

He hit the water hard, sank below the surface, eyes wide, ears flying up behind him.

Then, in a moment, he surfaced, paddled to the edge of the pool, scrabbled up and onto the deck.

The men playing cards turned and stared, but Zeus just shook off the water and raced for the beach.

Once there, he stopped and looked out over the water for a moment, trying to place himself.

He looked this way. That. Shook himself again. Looked again.

He stood very still a while, nose in the air, sniffing. He breathed deeply, again turned his head this way, that, this way again. Yes. Yes, it had to be this way. He knew now. This was the way. He was sure.

Almost sure.

He turned and headed down the beach, trotting briskly, head up, eyes front.

For a long time he continued his course along the beach, looking out to sea every so often for the dolphins. Nothing.

That was all right. He didn't mind. He knew he'd find her once he got back there.

It was hot on the beach, though, hotter than he'd ever been, and he was thirsty. He sat to rest a while, then got up and went on. After a while, the beach ended, the sand crisscrossed by canals and private beaches and huge, wide sweeping coves. Couldn't cross those. Impossible. He could never swim that far.

What to do?

He had to keep to the direction he had set for himself. He looked around, cut across the beach, and headed out to the road. There he stopped, sniffed, and breathed deeply, his face and nose up into the breeze. Yes. He found it, found his direction again.

It was a major road, a highway, and he headed directly along it. But he was thirstier than ever, hungry and tired, too. Yet he knew he had to keep going, knew if he sat or lay down to rest, he might not be able to get up again. His legs were weary, his paws hot on the pavement.

He tried to keep to the shade and the grass, but there was hardly any shade at all, and the little grass there was, was all burned up and dried. There was no food. No water. Most of all, no water.

But he had to go on. So he did. For an entire day and night he went, always heading in the direction his nose told him, finding a bit of food at truck stops, finding small streams of muddy water to help his thirst. But he began to get worried. He'd come so far, and he wasn't there yet.

And then another day, and he found himself passing railroad cars. His ears pricked up. Hop on one?

But no. They might not travel along the coast.

Nothing to do but keep going.

By the end of the second day he was almost dead with

hunger and fatigue. Suddenly, he saw something. Right there in front of him at a rest stop, he saw kids, a boat, and a car. Kids in a car that was pulling a boat.

If they were pulling a boat, they were taking it to the water, and they were heading the same direction he was. If there were kids, there'd be lots more stops at restaurants and rest rooms. If there were restaurant stops, there'd be food and water.

He could hardly believe his good luck.

Yes!

The family was just piling out of the car, heading for the restaurant. Zeus waited till everyone was of sight, then nosed around the restaurant parking lot, picking up bits of food, always watching the car so it wouldn't get away without him. He found half a hamburger and some fries that someone had dropped. He found a bit of ice cream that had fallen off a cone. He nosed at a partially overturned soda and lapped up the ice.

His heart was thumping wildly. He was in luck and he knew it.

When he was finished, he made a beeline for the boat trailer.

Looked around.

No one yet. They were still inside the restaurant.

He leaped into the boat and settled himself deep inside, where no one would see him. They'd never know they had a passenger.

It wasn't long before the car began moving. Zeus went with it, tummy full, able now to sleep and rest a while.

It was late and dark when they stopped driving, and Zeus had no idea how far he'd gone. He just knew that the trailer had stopped.

He popped up his head and looked around.

They were in the parking lot of a motel. He waited till the people were gone, then he leaped from the boat and out onto the street.

He sniffed the wind, sniffed hard. He was close to home, he could tell! He even thought he'd passed this motel once, when he was out just nosing around for something to do.

Yes! It was all familiar now. He found his direction again, and headed off into the night. He was closer now, definitely closer. Close to home. He could feel it, sense it, smell it all: Roxanne. The boat. Home. It was right up ahead.

Yes, there it was. Yes! The dock!

It was night now, almost dark, but he could see it, right there in front of him. And he could feel something, too. A presence.

With his last surge of energy, he bounded to the dock.

He looked around, yapped. Roxanne?

But no answer. No Roxanne. No Mary Beth.

Not now. He jumped from the dock onto the boat and nosed around. All was still, empty, no people, no dolphin.

Well, he'd wait for Mary Beth. It was night now, dark and still, but she'd come back in the morning. She always came back in the morning, and then they'd go to Roxanne.

But what was the presence he felt? He looked around, sniffed some more. Uneasy. It made him uneasy. Well, he'd figure it out. For now, the most important thing was water—food and water and then sleep. A deep, long sleep to rest his tired, torn paws. He nosed around the boat some more, around the cabinets and places he remembered where food was kept. But nothing. Not even crumbs. And no water.

All right. Back to town and the hamburger stand. There was always something there on the ground, in the trash.

Wearily, he leaped from the boat to the dock.

Right into Claude Carver's arms.

# Chapter
# 18

Jordan was frantic. Zeus was missing. His best friend was missing.

Life had never been so bad.

Even Terry's lousy music, even leaving Judith and Nora—nothing was as bad as losing his dog.

He'd searched up and down the beach, looking under the boardwalk, by all the restaurants and food courts, everywhere. He'd looked in the basement and laundry room of the condo, and he'd asked everybody he met.

Not a single soul had seen Zeus, except for four old guys playing cards by the pool. They claimed they'd seen Zeus jump off the balcony and into the pool. But where he'd gone after that, nobody knew.

Then in the middle of the night, suddenly Jordan knew. He was sure he knew.

He was mad at himself for not thinking of it earlier.

He knew exactly where Zeus was—or where he was

going. To Roxanne! How could he have been so dumb not to think of it before?

Jordan waited till it was a decent hour—at least until the sun was up. Then he picked up the portable phone, took it out on the deck. He turned and looked behind him. Terry was in the living room doing his Terry thing, plinking out a tune on the keyboard, a miserable, flat, lifeless tune. He'd been at it all night.

Jordan shook his head and dialed the phone, hoping that Mary Beth wouldn't pick it up.

Judith! It was Judith who answered. Well, Judith and Nora, too, each on a different extension. Jordan remembered how they always fought for the phone, but he couldn't even smile about it now.

He just blurted out his sad news. "It's me!" he said. "Zeus is missing."

"Oh, no!" Judith said.

"Oh, no!" Nora echoed.

"I know he's gone back there," Jordan said.

"You do?" Judith said. "How do you know?"

"Where else would he go? He'd never leave me."

"Oh," Judith said. She added, "Jordan?"

"What?" he said.

"We'll look," she said. "I promise. Nora and I. Right now. We'll look everywhere. Give me your number. We'll call you tonight."

"No," Jordan said. "Don't wait till tonight. Call later. I'll take the phone with me everywhere."

He looked into the living room, looked at his dad, still plinking away, jotting down notes. "I won't even let Terry use the phone till you call," Jordan said.

"Jordan?" Nora said. "If he's here, we'll find him. Don't worry."

"I know," Jordan said. "Start at the dock, okay? I know he'll be looking for Roxanne."

"Jordan?" Judith said sadly. "We've got news for you. Roxanne is gone, too."

"Gone?" Jordan said. "How could she be gone?"

"We think she's looking for Zeus," Nora said. "At least, that's what Judith and I think. Mom thinks . . . Well, Mom's pretty depressed. In fact, she said she's lost so much already. You know what? She blames herself about rushing Terry. But I guess we rushed it too, huh?"

"Yeah," Jordan said. He looked behind him again. "Terry's pretty depressed, too. Maybe you'd better not tell your mom I called."

"Jordan?" Nora said. "We'll cut school. But we've got to kind of be careful. See, we got in trouble. Got busted."

"Again?" Jordan said.

"It's a long story," Judith said. "We were at a party on a friend's boat. Only it turns out it wasn't really his boat. We'll tell you later."

"When I get there," Jordan said. "For now, just find Zeus."

"When you get here?" Judith said.

"I didn't mean that," Jordan said. "I just meant later. Tell me later. For now, just find Zeus, okay?"

He put down the phone, looked inside at Terry again. He thought about what he had said to Judith: when I get there. Why had he said that?

He paced up and down the deck, into his room and out, past Terry behind his earphones, plinking at the keyboard.

He looked at his watch. Looked again. Made some coffee for Terry.

When it was ready, he brought some to him, told him about Roxanne being missing. But for some reason, he didn't tell him what he was thinking about Zeus—that Zeus must have gone back there.

"I'm sorry," Terry said, but it was absentminded the way he said it, as if he wasn't really thinking about Roxanne at all. "You know what, Jordan?" he said without looking up. "This music is making me crazy."

Me, too, Jordan thought. He went back out on the deck. Looked at his watch.

Just an hour since he'd called, but he couldn't wait a minute longer. Surely, they'd had time to get to the dock and back.

He dialed, and right away Judith answered.

"It's me," Jordan said.

"Yes," Judith said. "I see."

Instantly, Jordan knew: Mary Beth was listening. Was in the room.

"Anything?" Jordan said.

"No. Nothing."

"I *know* he's trying to go back."

"That's unbelievable," Judith said. "I mean, like scary."

"You looked? At the dock?"

"Really."

Jordan nodded, picturing what was going on at the other end: Mary Beth frowning, wondering who it was, what they were saying.

He looked behind him at Terry, still plinking away. There was a sad, lost look on his face.

"Um, Judith," Jordan said. "The Terry Zone?"

"Yes?" she said.

"I think it's time to take drastic action," Jordan said.

117

"About?" Judith said.

"Terry. Your mom."

"I was thinking the same thing," Judith said.

"Is your mom as depressed as Terry?"

"Totally," Judith answered.

"Then let's do it," Jordan said.

"What do we have to lose?" Judith answered.

"That's what I thought," Jordan said. "Hold on."

"You, too," Judith said.

Jordan carried the portable to Terry. "Here," he said, speaking loud so Terry could hear from within his headphones. "It's Jane Freeman. From the record company."

"Really?" Terry said. He tore off the headphones, grabbed the phone. "Hey, gorgeous," he said. "I had a dream about you last night."

There was a pause on the other end of the phone. Then the voice came through clearly, even to Jordan, who was now halfway across the room, watching, listening. "You did?" the voice said.

"Yup," Terry said. "We went positively platinum."

There was another pause, and then Mary Beth said, "I had a dream, too, Terry. We went resoundingly tin."

Terry whirled around to glare at Jordan. But Jordan was just leaning back against the desk, smiling at him.

"Those kids just don't give up, do they?" Mary Beth said.

"No, they don't," Terry said. He frowned at Jordan again, but Jordan just had that innocent look.

"The girls told me about Zeus," Mary Beth said. "I'm sorry."

"Yeah," Terry said. "And Jordan just told me about Roxanne."

Mary Beth's voice had faded some, and Jordan moved closer to Terry. But Terry backed away.

Still, Jordan could hear. Mary Beth's voice carried very well, especially when she was mad. Or was she sad?

"She's very hurt," Mary Beth was saying.

"So's he," Terry answered.

"I'm sure she'll get over it," Mary Beth said.

"Really?" Terry said.

"Well," Mary Beth said. "I don't know. Maybe not." She sighed. "What about him?"

There was a long pause, and then Terry said, "It's a real difficult journey."

"Is it impossible?" Mary Beth said.

"I don't know," Terry answered.

"What should we do?" Mary Beth said.

Terry looked at Jordan.

Jordan looked back.

"Can we give it a little more time?" Terry said.

Jordan's shoulders slumped.

He whirled around, clamped his hands to his head, stamped off to his room.

Time! How much time did Terry need, anyway? Blowing his every opportunity. For happiness. For Mary Beth. Even for his music.

Jordan started going through his things. He had to figure out how much money he had, how much he'd need. And clothes, he had to pack clothes, his camera.

He began pulling things out, stuffing them in his backpack.

It wouldn't be easy getting an airline ticket, he knew that. Grown-ups always acted as if kids shouldn't be allowed to do anything on their own. But he'd had lots of practice being the grown-up. He knew how to do it, how to avoid eye contact, all those things you needed to know.

If Terry couldn't make sense of his own life, Jordan couldn't help it. He had done his best to help.

It was time now to do something for himself. For him and his best friend. He'd call Judith and Nora, and they'd meet him at the other end. If he had to take care of himself by himself, take care of finding Zeus on his own, without Terry, that was fine with him.

Well, sort of fine.

# Chapter 19

Claude Carver had a plan. He'd been working it out for weeks now, ever since everyone had been buzzing about the dumb dog and the dolphin. Dog and dolphin talking. Communicating. Ridiculous.

Except that Claude had overheard some of the communicating—heard it with his own ears. And it wasn't ridiculous. In fact, it was amazing. It would make a fine research application, a fine research grant.

If Mary Beth wouldn't cooperate on the grant, well . . .

He smiled to himself. He'd just do it on his own. Of course, it meant he had to do some unheard-of things. But then, no guts, no glory.

Glory for Dr. Claude Carver!

And here, right at his feet, was his chance at glory. How come nobody else had realized that this dumb mutt would find his way back here? Claude had known.

He'd known all along. It was all part of his plan. He'd just been waiting.

Claude smiled down at Zeus, under the net that had been draped over him and had held him fast and tight for the past twelve hours.

"Welcome back, my little friend," he said. "Welcome back."

He looked behind him at Phil and Linda. It was Sunday morning, but he had summoned them anyway. He couldn't wait for Monday. Couldn't risk that Mary Beth would get to Zeus first.

Now there was just one other part of his plan to be completed: Roxanne.

He glanced at an old worker, Floyd, who was bent over, scrubbing the deck of the boat; then he looked back at Phil and Linda.

He smiled at them. "Now Roxanne is ours," he said softly, gleefully. "We have the dog; we'll get Roxanne."

Phil looked down at Zeus, a pained look on his face.

"All right," Claude said. "Let's get started. We can get Roxanne into our pens for a while and keep her from fleeing. Zeus will coax her to us. Then we can see how she and the dog work." He looked down at Zeus. "And Mary Beth can forget her compassionate reintroduction study," he added with a laugh.

"Claude?" Phil said quietly.

Claude looked at him.

"It's totally illegal to catch a dolphin in the open sea," Phil said.

There was a long moment's silence while Claude stared at Phil. Then Claude said, his voice cold, flat, "Excuse me, Phil?"

122

Phil didn't answer. But Linda did. "Phil's right," she said.

"I am," Phil said. "So the answer is no."

"No?" Claude said. "What do you mean, no?"

"No," Phil said. "No, we're not helping you."

Claude turned to Linda.

"No for me, too," she said. "Because we quit. That's what *no* means. You're on your own."

She and Phil turned and walked off the dock, back into the building.

"Fools!" Claude shouted after them. "Fools. You could have been part of scientific history! Come back."

But they didn't.

Claude bent then and scooped Zeus up into his arms. Zeus growled ominously, but he didn't put up much of a struggle. He was still too weak from the trip, and Claude had given him very little food overnight. Nevertheless, he growled low, trying to nip at Claude. But it was no use. He was too tired.

Claude looked around. Help, he needed help. He needed at least one more person on board, one person to man the nets that would catch Roxanne, another to hold this mutt and work the controls.

The only person in sight was the worker, Floyd, and he was old. Old and none too steady looking.

"You!" Claude said imperiously, pointing. "How would you like to be part of scientific history?"

Floyd turned to Claude, looked at him, looked at the dog in his arms. He didn't speak, just gave him a long, steady stare.

"Or would you prefer money?" Claude said, sarcastically.

For another long minute, Floyd continued to stare back. "Lots of money," he said softly.

"Then do it," Claude said. "Can you handle the controls on a boat?"

Floyd just nodded, gave another of those level stares, then boarded the boat.

Claude climbed aboard after him and set Zeus down. He attached a leash to Zeus's collar, then looped it over the rail of the boat. No sense chancing that the dumb mutt would try to leap overboard and swim away.

When they were both settled in, Floyd took the controls, handling them as if he'd been doing it his whole life, as Claude went forward to the scanner equipment.

He bent over the scanner, fiddled with some dials. Listened. Watched.

It took only a moment before he began to smile. "Aha!" he said.

He laid a finger on the scanner, tracing a blipping dot. A moving dot.

Everybody had said Roxanne was gone! Shows what they knew. Just as they hadn't thought of the dog, they hadn't counted on his nets controlling Roxanne.

He smiled to himself again.

So here she was. If she had somehow escaped, she'd returned.

Claude frowned. Maybe she did know when Zeus had come back? Maybe she was even smarter than he'd thought?

Maybe his research grant would be even bigger than he thought?

Claude smiled again. He knew how to control these creatures. Science. All in the name of science.

124

He put a finger on the dot, moving slowly now on the screen, coming closer to the center marks that crisscrossed like a graph on the screen. "There she is," he said.

He looked down at Zeus, who growled.

"What's the matter, mongrel?" Claude said. "I thought you'd be ecstatic."

Zeus just growled again, low in his throat.

Suddenly, the dot on the screen began to move more swiftly, moving closer to the center mark where the lines intersected. The spot where they'd catch her.

Quickly, Claude turned to Floyd.

"Go!" he shouted. "Full throttle. North by northeast. Thirty-eight degrees. Ready the nets!"

Zeus began to whine—worried, anxious whining.

He strained at his leash.

As the boat shot forward, so too did the dot, moving toward them, straight on toward them.

Then, as Claude and Floyd leaped to the nets, Zeus began to howl, a wild, mournful wail.

But Claude and Floyd were oblivious, tugging on the mechanism that controlled the nets on the front of their boat. On the radar screen, the dot that was Roxanne was even closer, right in the center. Right beside them.

When Floyd had the nets fully unfurled, Claude yelled, "Okay. Drop them. Drop them and drag them alongside. Now."

Roxanne wasn't visible yet, but she was there. Right under water. Right beside them. The radar screen was telling them everything. She was coming right up to them.

They heard her then. She began calling, making her familiar, blatting, squawking sound.

125

Zeus howled even louder, then began barking again. Wild, frantic yapping.

And then, there she was. She surfaced, right beside the boat. Right beside Zeus. Her huge majestic head appeared, her eyes wide and beautiful and clear, looking right into Zeus's eyes.

Instantly, Zeus stopped barking. He stayed perfectly still, looking at her.

She looked back.

Still.

Silent.

For a long moment they looked into each other's eyes.

Floyd and Claude watched silently, barely breathing.

Quietly, stealthily then, Floyd began manipulating the huge spring mechanism of the net, turning it, drawing it closer.

Roxanne made a sound. Small. Quiet. *Blat? Squawk?* Questioning.

Zeus answered. Barked. Loud. Wild.

Claude nodded at Floyd.

Floyd tightened the net, drew it around under Roxanne. Around her. Tightening it.

Roxanne blatted again, another questioning sound.

Zeus barked again. Louder. Wilder.

Then, as though a message had been given and received, suddenly Roxanne leaped from the water, leaped high. Water flew from her back and the sun shone on her, glistening drops shimmering off her sides. Fairly flying, Roxanne skimmed across the surface of the water. Avoiding the falling, encircling net, she dove. And disappeared.

"Missed her!" Claude shouted. He turned to Zeus. "Get her back here!" he shouted. "Get her back now!"

Zeus braced his legs, barked defiantly, his teeth inches from Claude's leg.

Within moments, Roxanne reappeared, on the other side of the boat this time.

She looked at Zeus. *Pop? Blat?* She questioned.

Claude once more jumped to the nets, Floyd following.

Zeus barked again, wild, frantic. He seemed almost crazed in his wild barking, leaping and straining against his chain.

Roxanne only came closer.

"Yes!" Claude yelled, exuberant. "Yes. Now! Bring up the nets."

Floyd did as he was told.

Just then Roxanne made a flying leap. Across the ship. Hitting the mechanism. Sending men and machine and dolphin into a tangle of flippers and arms and legs. And nets.

# Chapter
# 20

The first thing Terry noticed when he awoke that morning was that there was no coffee aroma floating in to him the way there usually was. When he stumbled out to the kitchen, still not fully awake, he saw that the coffee machine was cold, silent, that Jordan hadn't started it for him. There was something else odd, too— the house was too quiet. There wasn't a sound from Jordan. No Jordan banging around, taking pictures, cooking. No Jordan at all. And the light on the answering machine was blinking at him. He didn't remember hearing the phone ring. If it had rung, why hadn't Jordan answered?

With a tight feeling growing in his chest, Terry pushed the button on the machine.

Jordan's voice came to him, Jordan in a place filled with background noise, like a mall, or a train station or a . . .

"Terry?" Jordan was saying, "Terry, it's me, Jordan. I've gone to look for Zeus."

"You've *what!*" Terry yelled at the machine, then forced himself to be quiet, to listen.

"Don't worry," Jordan was saying. "I'll call again. Oh, and Terry, the coffee's in the machine, ready to go. Just press the button."

Then Jordan's voice was gone, but not before Terry had figured out the background noise. It wasn't a mall or a train station, not at all. It was an airport! Jordan was calling from the airport.

Quickly, Terry pushed the rewind button, listened to the tape again.

He heard Jordan's voice but heard something else, something he strained to listen for in the background noise. It was an announcement that the American Eagle flight to Key West had been delayed. Boarding would be in about thirty minutes—boarding to Key West, where Mary Beth and Nora and Judith were. Key West where Jordan was surely heading now.

Terry didn't wait to hear the rest.

He ran to his room, threw on some clothes, threw a few things in a suitcase. Then he was out of there. He raced outside and grabbed a taxi to take him to the airport.

He settled in the taxi, his mind spinning, racing. Jordan! Jordan was going, on his own, trying for something, something that was important to him. His dog.

Jordan couldn't be left to do it alone. He was too young to be on his own.

All the way to the airport, as the cab inched its way through traffic, Terry kept looking at his watch, his mind racing, worrying, frantic. He, Terry, he knew about going after a dream. He knew about going after something important. How could he have ignored his son, not thought more about him? Jordan had lost his mom. He'd lost his new friends. And now he'd lost his dog.

Silently, Terry blamed himself, over and over. He promised himself, if I just get there in time, if I make it in time, he promised himself, I'll be a better father. I'll pay more attention. I'll be a dad. A good one.

It seemed like forever, the cab starting and stopping and stopping some more, but they were finally at the airport. Terry checked his watch again. Twenty-six minutes since he'd heard the announcement. He thrust some money at the cab driver and ran pell mell through the airport to the American Eagle counter. He looked up at the monitor. The Key West flight sign was flashing, indicating that the plane was boarding.

Terry ran to the counter, pulling out his wallet as he ran.

Yes, there were still seats available, he was told. Did he have a credit card? Did he have proper ID?

Terry pulled out his documents, drummed his fingers on the counter as the ticketing process went on, slowly, slowly. Finally though, it was complete, and he threw his bag on the security machine, then hustled through the gate. Yes, he'd made it! They were still boarding. And there—there in the boarding lounge was Jordan. Jordan just shouldering his pack, entering the line for the flight.

Still breathing hard, Terry moved into line behind Jordan. With a whispered prayer of thanks, he put a hand on Jordan's shoulder.

Jordan turned, looked up. His shoulders drooped.

"I'm meat," he said.

Terry just looked at him, a long look. "We'll discuss that later," he said. "Right now, the question I have is, is the seat next to you taken?"

For another long minute, Jordan just looked at his dad. Then, slowly, he smiled. "No," he said. "No, it's not."

"Good," his dad said, smiling back at him. "I'm glad."

It was a short flight, and neither of them said much, each absorbed in his own thoughts. But just after landing and deplaning, as they were walking through the airport, Terry turned to Jordan.

"Jordan," Terry said. "I want you to know that we're going to do everything we can to find Zeus."

Jordan nodded.

"But, Jordan," Terry went on, "it's extremely unlikely he made it down here."

Jordan made a little face, shrugged. "Zeus is an extremely extreme dog," he said.

Terry sighed. "That he is," he said.

"He's also in love," Jordan said.

Terry gave Jordan a look, shook his head, then turned and began walking. "An extreme emotion," Terry said.

"Try it, Dad," Jordan murmured.

Terry stopped, swung around, looked at his son.

"It's okay," Jordan said softly. "It really is."

For a long moment, they looked at one another. Slowly, Terry began to smile.

Jordan smiled back.

Terry grabbed Jordan tightly in his arms and hugged him. Just like that. Right there, right in public, both of them grinning widely. Just as Nora and Judith came running up to greet them.

131

# Chapter
# 21

Back at the bay, Mary Beth was preparing to do something she knew she shouldn't do. She knew it. All of her training, all of her experience, told her that what she was doing was wrong. It was stupid. It was risky. It was downright dangerous. One must never, never, never go down in a submersible alone. Well, alone perhaps, but never go down without others nearby, others who knew one's whereabouts. Never, never, never. It was the primary rule of diving, and Mary Beth knew it. It had been drilled into her over and over again, ever since she first began these underwater maneuvers.

But all of her common sense seemed to have fled. Roxanne was out there. Alone. And Claude had drift nets out. Becky had called to tell her that a dolphin had been found dead in a net—not Roxanne, thank goodness, not Roxanne!—but Mary Beth knew that Roxanne could be next. Even though Roxanne hadn't shown herself since Zeus left, Mary Beth was certain that

Roxanne was still hanging about somewhere. After all, she was used to this place, to these people. She had even begun a relationship with Mary Beth. Surely she would return. It was up to Mary Beth to find her now before the nets ensnared her. It was up to Mary Beth to save Roxanne.

But dive alone? The voices of long-ago teachers and trainers seemed to ring in her ears: dive alone? That's berserk!

I have to! she answered the voices. I'll be all right.

But as she readied the submersible, put on her wet-suit, she couldn't rid herself of the thoughts running round and round in her head. She was a mother. She had two girls to worry about.

Yes. But nothing was going to happen. She'd be all right. She always had been. Why should anything be different this time? After all—she straightened up, looked around her and out to sea—after all, wasn't she responsible for Roxanne, too?

She took a deep breath, put up the diving flag—a concession to her old teachers—and settled herself into the sub. Then she sealed it up and began the dive.

As always, when she was first under water, the pure beauty of the undersea almost overwhelmed her. She could feel her heart beating hard and fast at how amazing it all was—the deep blue of the water, the spectacular coral reefs she floated between, the fish. Heavens! There were zillions of fish, and the colors— reds, greens, brilliant yellows, and oranges, some of the fish spotted, some striped, huge fish and tiny ones. They all seemed intent on a journey, some rushing past, some just drifting past. Some were so small and swift that they seemed like tiny arrows that flew across her field of vision; others were big and lazy looking. For just a moment, Mary Beth forgot her worries, even forgot her fears over what she was doing, and allowed herself to breathe in the mystery of it all.

She smiled as the sub drifted past a coral reef bursting with life, smiled at a huge yellow fish that for a moment halted on its journey and peered in at her, as though wondering what she was doing in this place.

After allowing herself that moment, it was time for work. She adjusted the scanner, listened, watched. Roxanne could still be traced by sonar, but there was no blip, no nothing on the screen.

"Where are you, sweetheart?" Mary Beth whispered.

She adjusted the controls, moved the sub forward a bit.

"Come on, Roxanne," she whispered again. "I know you're down here somewhere. And I need you. No. You need me."

She frowned at the scanner, leaned closer to it. Had she heard something, a ping, a sound? Had she seen a blip—just for a moment?

Nothing.

She looked out the window again, smiled at a huge red fish swimming by, its tail seeming to wave at her.

She turned back to the scanner. "There are nets out there, Roxanne," she whispered. "You don't know it, but I do. And if you get caught . . ."

Suddenly, the sub rocked violently, and she sucked in her breath.

"Oh, no!" she whispered. "No!"

She could feel her heart thud hard in her chest, feel

the fear close her throat. What? What was that? What had caused that movement?

Again the sub rocked, lurched sideways, as if it had a mind of its own. It swung around, and there was a huge banging, scraping sound, loud, harsh, the certain sound, Mary Beth knew, of the sub being impaled on a coral reef.

She closed her eyes for a moment, took a deep breath. Okay. Okay, don't panic, she told herself. It's just a coral reef. You can make your way off it. It's not that hard.

She opened her eyes, breathed deeply, and then gently, she moved the controls forward.

Nothing.

The sub didn't move.

She tried again.

Nothing. It didn't move, not even an inch.

Why? What was this? What had happened? Yes, she was on a coral reef, but why couldn't she maneuver the sub off?

She took another deep breath. Okay, move the controls the other way, she told herself. If it wouldn't go forward, she could move it backward. She pushed on the control, fiddled with it, urged it to go backward. But the sub didn't move, didn't move at all.

Not forward. Not backward.

She was stuck, the sub was stuck.

"This isn't happening," she whispered to herself. "It isn't."

She forced herself to breathe deeply, taking long, easy breaths. Okay, she thought, it's okay. Maybe it's just tangled in something. I can free it. Just take a breath, move the controls slowly, carefully, ease it forward, ease

135

it back, rock your way out of this, whatever it is. She smiled, remembering times she had been in cars stuck in snow: rock the car forward, back, forward, back. Easy, free it of what's holding it.

"Ready?" she whispered, as though there were someone else there, someone besides herself to talk to. "Let's try again."

She did. Moved the controls, forward, backward, forward, backward, nice and easy. But there was no movement from the sub. None at all.

Beginning to feel fear well up, panic almost, she pushed harder on the controls.

Nothing.

"No," she whispered. "No, no no."

She leaned forward and peered out the window. That's when she saw them. Nets. The propellor was tangled in a huge net, the very drift net that had made her fear for Roxanne's life.

Now she feared for her own.

No. She wouldn't even think that.

Instead, she forced herself to think calmly, to take stock, assess this situation. She breathed deeply, slowly, telling herself to think and plan. She looked at her watch. She had enough time left, enough air. But if she was firmly stuck, if she couldn't budge the sub, there was just one other thing to do: She'd have to open the hatch, push her way out, and swim up to the surface. It would be tricky, but she could do it.

Yes, she was deep in the water, but not that deep. She was a strong swimmer. She could do it.

But first, get the hatch open. She paused for a minute, getting ready. Because once she'd done that—opened the hatch—there would be little time. Water would begin to flood in. It would be just minutes before the sub would fill with water. In those few minutes, she had to make her way out and swim. Swim as if her life depended on it.

For a moment then, she actually laughed out loud. *As if* her life depended on it! It *did* depend on it.

She peered out the window, looked at the nets. They were huge, thick, ropelike affairs, big enough, strong enough to hold thousands of pounds of dolphin strength. She prayed that they weren't encircling the hatch, holding that tight, too. Were they?

She pressed her nose to the glass, tried to look upward. But she couldn't see, couldn't tell.

She took another deep breath. Nothing to do but open it and try. Even if the hatch was ensnared by the nets, she still had to try. She'd run out of air soon enough.

She closed her eyes for a moment. Thought of her girls. Nora. Judith. She felt tears swim to her eyes and blinked them back.

Time enough for that later. For now, she had to do what she had to do.

She stood up, grabbed the handle of the hatch, turned it.

She heard the click as it turned, and then, with her hand pressed against the hatch, she pushed.

It gave. It did. It opened!

But just inches. Just inches.

She pushed some more.

Please. Please. Open!

Water was slowly seeping in.

Please, she prayed, please.

With all her strength, she leaned against the hatch opening, pushing, forcing the hatch open. But it didn't open. It didn't budge. It was firmly held closed—closed, but for those few inches. Held tight by the nets.

Just water. Water seeping slowly into the sub, in, in, water that would crowd her out, would take all her air. Water that she knew would take her life away.

# Chapter
# 22

When Jordan and Terry, Nora and Judith, arrived at the dock, it was clear that something was wrong. Very wrong. Becky was standing on the dock alongside Phil and Linda, and the look on her face was grim—grim and scared. Beside her, the place where Mary Beth moored the *Daily Planet* was empty.

"Where's Mom?" Judith called.

Becky pointed to the water. "Out there," she said, "looking for Roxanne. Trying to keep her safe. If she can do it."

"Safe?" Terry said. "Safe from what?"

"Claude," Becky said. "Zeus is out there, too."

"Zeus?" Jordan yelled. "Zeus is? With Mary Beth? I knew he'd find her—"

"No!" Becky interrupted. "Not with Mary Beth. Zeus is on Claude Carver's boat. Claude's using Zeus for bait. He's looking for Roxanne, too."

"Bait?" Jordan said, puzzled. "Bait for Roxanne?"

Becky nodded. She glared at Phil and Linda. "To capture her. Put her in a tank. To—"

"Can we use that boat?" Terry interrupted. He pointed to one of the cabin cruisers moored nearby. "Now?" There was an urgency in his voice.

"Be my guest," Becky answered.

"Come on, guys!" Terry shouted.

The four of them piled onto the cruiser, as Terry revved it up.

"Hang tight," he said, as he pulled it away from the dock and opened up the throttle to full.

They sped away from the complex, out into the bay, all four of them scanning the surface of the water, looking for Mary Beth's boat.

And Claude's.

Terry tried to keep calm as he navigated, staying intent on his job while the kids scanned the horizon. But he couldn't help thinking: Zeus. Roxanne. They were in danger. And Mary Beth? Was she in danger, too? Just how dangerous was Claude Carver?

Behind Terry, Jordan was thinking, too, thinking and praying. Over and over he prayed: Let me get Zeus back, let him be okay, let me get him back. Followed by a gleeful thought: I knew he'd do it, I knew he'd make it here.

Then Jordan had a scarier thought: What would Claude do to Zeus? Mary Beth told him Zeus had fallen in once, told him about sharks. Suppose Claude got Roxanne, trapped her? Would he then be finished with Zeus? Would he then feed Zeus to the sharks?

No, he needed Zeus. Unless . . .

Suddenly, Judith pointed. "There!" she said, squinting at a dot on the blue water. "Isn't that Mom's boat?"

140

They all turned and looked.

"Yes," Nora said. "Yes, it is."

Terry steered toward it, straight toward it.

It took just a few minutes, and when they were close, Terry slowed, then moved alongside.

"Mom?" Judith called. "Mom? You there?"

No answer.

Terry dropped anchor, then got busy tying up, and in a minute, all four of them climbed from the cruiser onto Mary Beth's boat.

"Mom?" Judith yelled again.

They all stood quietly, listening.

Nothing. It was quiet still. No sign of Mary Beth. No sign of anyone.

"Mom?" Nora repeated.

Judith and Nora ran down below to check for her, as Jordan ran around to the other side of the boat. Then he looked up and saw it—the mini-sub was gone, the platform empty. And the dive flag waved in the air, signaling that someone was down there.

"It's okay," Jordan called. "Over here. See," he added, when the others joined him. "She's down in the sub."

Terry frowned. "How long can she stay down there?"

"Forty-five minutes," Jordan answered.

"How long has she been down, I wonder?" Nora said.

All three of them looked at her. Shrugged. No one knew.

Terry looked at his watch, anxious.

"No big deal," Judith said. "Mom always goes down."

"Not alone, she doesn't," Nora answered. "It's against all the rules."

"Unless she had to," Judith said.

141

"Had to?" Terry said.

"Yeah. Mom told us last week," Judith said. "You know about drift nets? Mom might be trying to protect Roxanne."

"Or to free her if she's trapped," Nora added.

"Wouldn't that be dangerous?" Terry asked.

Nobody answered. But they all knew the answer, and it was yes.

For the next few minutes, nobody spoke. But one after the other, they checked their watches. Again. And again.

Terry kept scanning the surface of the water, then leaning over the side of the boat and peering down into the water, as if he could see the sub or even Roxanne.

Nervously then, he fiddled with the gear on board— checked the tool box, opened it and closed it, played with a fish-cleaning knife, hefting it from one hand to the other.

Again, he checked his watch. Fifteen minutes since they'd boarded here. So another half hour at most. Surely, the sub would surface, would show itself. But what if it didn't? Then what? They couldn't just wait and hope, but what else was there to do?

Suddenly, something moved on the water. A ripple. A wave. The water was definitely disturbed. Mary Beth's sub surfacing? Or was he imagining it?

Terry put up a hand to shade his eyes, peered hard across the moving, glistening water. No, he wasn't imagining it. Something was moving, disturbing the water. Yes! Something was coming to them, but it wasn't Mary Beth.

Roxanne! She was fairly flying to them, skimming the surface of the water, zooming right in on them.

"Roxanne!" Jordan yelled.

In moments, she was right alongside them. *Blat! Squawk!* She made popping sounds at them. *Blat! Squawk. Pop.*

"You're here!" Nora yelled.

"You did it!" Judith yelled. "You didn't get trapped in the nets."

Judith reached out, as if she'd touch Roxanne's head, but Roxanne backed up, blatting powerfully. She kept it up, squawking at them, not playfully the way she usually did, but wild, restless.

"Hey, what's the matter?" Jordan said. "Oh, I know. You want Zeus. I do, too. But we'll find him. Promise."

But even Zeus's name didn't seem to calm her. She looked away from Jordan, homed in on Terry, looking him right in the face.

He smiled at her. "My music?" he said. "I left it home."

*Squawk! Blat! Pop!* Her eyes got wider—wild. *Pop! Blat! Squawk!* The sounds were louder, frantic, restless, wild.

Terry frowned at her. "What is it?" he said softly.

She made a new sound then—mournful. A cry. She looked in Terry's face once more. Then she suddenly dove and disappeared.

Terry looked at his watch.

Twenty-seven minutes since they'd been here.

He looked back at the place where Roxanne had disappeared.

Suddenly, he jumped up, tore off his shirt, his shoes. "I get it!" he said. "Stay here!" he yelled at the kids.

He dove into the water and disappeared.

Under water it was dark, but he could see Roxanne, just ahead of him.

143

Then he saw something else. Something awesome. Something awful.

Something terrifying.

Mary Beth. Mary Beth in the sub, the sub that was tangled in a drift net, propellors tangled, unable to move. The hatch, her escape door, was partway opened. But only partway. She must have tried to escape, but the door was caught by the net, too, snagged half open, half shut. There wasn't enough room for her to swim out, but there was plenty of room for the water to be pouring slowly in.

Through the window, he could see Mary Beth watching him wide-eyed, water seeping up around her. She made frantic motions, the water already up to her neck.

Terry swam to the sub, grabbed at the net, pulled hard. Nothing. He couldn't budge it. It totally entangled the sub, was snagged tight on the hatch cover.

He tugged at it, again. And again.

Then Terry was out of breath—out of air.

Wildly, he kicked, swam to the surface.

There, he gripped the sides of the boat, gasping, filling his lungs with air.

"A knife!" he shouted to Jordan. "Throw me the knife!"

Without a word, Jordan scrambled for the tool box, grabbed the huge fish-scaling knife. Tossed it to Terry.

Terry grabbed it. Filled his lungs once more with air. And dove again.

Under water, he saw Roxanne, still there, hovering nervously, watching him, her eyes fixed on his.

He swam to the side of the sub.

Inside the sub, water had reached Mary Beth's face,

almost to her mouth. She was tilting her head, raising her chin, trying desperately to keep above the water.

Panic. Panic in her eyes.

Terry slashed at the net. Slashed again. And again. And again.

His lungs were bursting, but he couldn't swim up. No time. She'd drown. In the two minutes it would take, she'd be drowned.

He looked at Mary Beth, at Roxanne, and then, with the last of his strength—and maybe courage—he slashed once more at the net holding the hatch stuck.

The net split.

Mary Beth pushed.

The hatch gave way.

Together, Mary Beth pushing, Terry pulling, she was free.

Free!

They fought their way to the surface.

Roxanne, too.

All together.

# Chapter
# 23

The day had finally arrived. Everyone was ready and happy. Even Zeus and Roxanne seemed happy.

Jordan looked around him at the guests beginning to gather in Mary Beth's backyard, at Nora and Judith, dressed and nervously awaiting their mother's appearance. At Zeus, washed and brushed, dressed up for the day.

Jordan put a hand on Zeus's neck, pulled him close.

It hadn't really taken that long for all this to happen—only about a week. It just seemed long, maybe because of all that had happened. Claude had been arrested, once they had found his boat and gotten him untangled from his own nets, and they'd rescued Zeus, who was recovering from sore feet. Roxanne was hanging around again, busily conversing with Zeus every chance they got.

Best of all—well, second best—Mary Beth had received her grant. The big one. The important one. The Rockland grant.

The best—the really best—was this day. This wedding. Of course, it might have taken even longer if Jordan and Nora and Judith hadn't taken things into their own hands.

Jordan turned now, looked at Nora and Judith, smiled. Sisters!

They looked back, smiled.

"We need to have a little talk," Nora mouthed at him. She was laughing, and Jordan laughed, too. It had become a kind of secret password with all three of them.

He remembered the first time Nora had said that—to Terry—just a week ago.

"About what?" Terry had said.

Judith—it was Judith who put it in words for all of them—had said, "We believe, with all that's happened, it's clearly established that you *do* like our mom." When Terry had nodded, she added, "Enough to marry her?"

"Next Sunday?" Jordan had said.

And so it was. And so the day had come. Now the music began, and Jordan scrambled to the back to escort his dad.

He looked up at Terry in his new clothes, took in his smile, his nervous smile.

"Happy?" Jordan asked quietly.

Terry nodded. "Very," he said. "You?"

"Extremely," Jordan answered.

"Me, too," Terry said. "Extremely."

"Told you love was an extreme emotion," Jordan said.

"No," Terry answered. "I told you!"

With that, the music swelled, and Terry and Jordan walked to the front. Then Mary Beth, accompanied by Nora and Judith, came to stand with them. And the minister did his minister thing.

Watching, listening, as the solemn vows were said, Jordan felt his heart do something weird. It got filled up or something.

His eyes, too.

Family. That's what he kept thinking. My family.

It only took moments for the ceremony to be over, and when Mary Beth spoke, she said the very words Jordan had been thinking.

"Family," she said softly, looking at each of them, Zeus, too. "We're family."

Jordan blinked, turned away, looked out over the water.

Roxanne! She was there, like another guest at the wedding. Behind her, not far behind her, was a pod of dolphins.

Had she really joined them? No, they were still at a distance.

Suddenly, Zeus bounded away from them and raced to the edge of the water.

He began barking, a polite, quiet bark, as if he was respecting the solemnity of the wedding.

Roxanne answered, blatting, popping, but she didn't seem to think things were too solemn, because she sounded wild, happy.

Zeus barked again, yapped, howled.

Roxanne answered, blats, squawks, pops!

"Listen to them!" Judith said. "They're talking."

"No kidding," Nora answered.

"Anyone know what they're saying?" Terry asked, softly.

Mary Beth turned to him. "I think," she said, "Zeus is telling Roxanne it's time."

"Time to what?" Terry said.

Judith and Nora looked at one another, then at Jordan. All three turned to Terry and Mary Beth—their parents.

"I think I know," Terry said softly.

"To trust again," Mary Beth said.

"And about time, too," Jordan muttered.

Terry reached for him, but Jordan ducked away, smiling.

He pointed.

Roxanne had suddenly turned away from the dock and was swimming toward the pod of dolphins. Straight to them.

"There she goes," Terry said. "Joining her family."

He put his arm around Mary Beth then, and with the other arm pulled in Jordan, Nora, Judith.

All five of them hugged, a family hug. Then they turned and watched as, with Zeus barking his approval, Roxanne swam away—and joined her family.

Everybody was getting in on the act.

# About the Author

PATRICIA HERMES has taught English at the high school and junior high school levels and has taught gifted and talented programs in the grade schools. She travels frequently throughout the country, speaking at schools and conferences to students, teachers, educators, and parents. The mother of five children, she lives and works in New England.

Among her many awards are the California Young Reader Medal, the Pine Tree Book Award, and the Hawaii Nene Award. Her books have also been named IRA/CBC Children's Choices and Notable Children's Trade Books in the field of Social Studies.